# GATEWAY HOUSE
## A Western Story

# GATEWAY HOUSE
## A Western Story

## Wayne D. Overholser

Five Star
Unity, Maine

Five Star First Edition Western Series.
Published in 2001 in conjunction with Golden West Literary Agency.

Set in 11 pt. Plantin by Myrna S. Raven.

Printed in the United States on permanent paper.

**Library of Congress Cataloging-in-Publication Data**

Overholser, Wayne D., 1906 –
    Gateway house : a Western story / by Wayne D.
Overholser.
        p. cm.
    ISBN 0-7862-2389-8 (hc : alk. paper)
    1. Treasure-trove — Fiction.  I. Title.
PS3529.V33 G37  2001
    813′.54—dc21                                     00-054256

# Gateway House
## A Western Story

# Chapter One

Ed Morgan rode into Montrose with the last of the evening scarlet fading in the west. He sat slack in the saddle, bone-weary, a fine sprinkle of alkali dust covering his stubble-dark face and clothes and his buckskin gelding. He had not spared himself or the horse on the long ride south from the upper Laramie, for the mail that had brought his brother Ben's letter had been slow, and Ed had not been able to shake the haunting fear that he was too late.

Lights had come to life along Main Street. The July night was warm, and men stood in groups on the plank walks, idly talking, none of them paying any attention to Ed as he slowly rode the length of the street, hoping he would see Ben.

Montrose was young, for the Ute reservation had been opened to settlement only a few years before, and it was still something of a boom town, with a fluctuating population, depending on the season. Located on the narrow gauge, it was the principal shipping point for the mines in the San Juans. Probably most of the men on the street were freighters, miners, or promoters of one sort or another, all headed for the mining country. As Ed's gaze touched one unfamiliar face after another, he began to wonder if he had any chance of finding Ben in a crowd like this.

It had been six years since Ben had left home, and four of those had been spent in prison. Now that Ed was here, he was almost afraid to see his brother, afraid of the changes the years had brought. He had never been able to talk any sense into the boy when he'd been home. If he failed again, he would not have another chance. Knowing Ben, he was as certain of that as a man could be certain of anything.

He reached the end of the business block, then turned

7

back, reined into a livery stable, and dismounted. When the hostler came along the runway to him, he asked: "Is there a man named Ben Morgan in town?"

The hostler peered at him in the lantern light. He said impatiently: "How the hell would I know? There's a lot of men in this town."

"Just thought you might have heard the name."

"Nope. They come in all the time, stay one night, and head out in the morning. Or the other way around. Far as I know, most of 'em don't have no names."

"Ben would stay more'n one night."

The hostler shrugged. "Sorry, friend. I can't help you."

"Take care of him." Ed motioned to the buckskin. "I'll pick up my war sack later."

He swung through the archway and into the street, and paused there to roll a cigarette. He would have to check every hotel and saloon in town. If he didn't find Ben. . . . His thoughts could not reach beyond that point. He would have had his ride for nothing, and he would have failed Ben, who had asked for help.

For a moment Ed stood motionless, listening to the hum of talk that ran along the street, the tinny racket of a cheap piano from a saloon to his left, the shot that broke suddenly into the dissonance of sound. Ed wheeled toward it, thinking it would be like Ben to get into a gun ruckus. Then he stopped as men's boot heels hammered on the plank walk, and someone shouted: "It's that crazy Mike Bellew again."

Another man said: "Where the hell is the marshal?"

The tension that had gripped Ed left him. He realized he had been expecting the worst, that he had still been picturing Ben as a wild kid with a gift for getting into trouble. Actually the Ben he'd meet would be a stranger. Ed wouldn't know what to say or what to do when he did find Ben. He simply had no way of knowing what four years of prison had done to Ben.

He was wasting time standing here. He should be looking for Ben. But still he stood there, smoking his cigarette as he worried about what he'd say. He could be the bossy, older brother again, which was exactly what Ben would expect. He could say: "Come on back to the Triangle M and work your tail off like I've done since I was a kid. You've had your fun, and see what it got you. Now come home with me and behave."

But it wasn't any good. No good at all. Ben had left home to get away from work. Or maybe Ed's control. No, Ben wouldn't be coming back. He'd been nineteen when he'd left, brash and impudent and restless, hating orders and hating hard work. Now he was twenty-five. Prison might have broken him. And then again it might have made him worse, bitter and vindictive and wanting only to get even with the men who had convicted him.

Ed flipped his cigarette stub into the street and turned to his right. Now that he was here, he had to face it. He'd take his cue from what Ben would say. The boy had never asked for help before in his life. Boy? Hell, Ben was twenty-five now. Ed had to keep reminding himself of that.

He walked past a store, came to a hotel, and stepped into the lobby. He asked the clerk: "Got a man staying here named Ben Morgan?"

"Never heard of him," the clerk said.

"Thanks," Ed said, and wheeled back into the street.

He went on to the end of the block, looking into every saloon he passed. He crossed the street, wading through the deep, white dust that would become a sticky mass of gumbo with the first rain, and entered the lobby of the hotel on the corner. This time when he asked for Ben, the clerk nodded, eyeing Ed gravely.

"Yeah, he's here," the man said, "but he ain't gonna be around long."

Something was wrong. It was there in the somber quality of the man's face, in the hard set of his mouth as if he regretted having let Ben have a room. Ed crossed the lobby to the desk, feeling both relief and worry.

"What's the matter?" Ed asked.

"Everything. He's sick. Cashing in, I reckon. We got him to bed and had a doctor to see him. No use. Hell, he was dying on his feet when he walked in. Owes me for his room. I won't get it, neither, the way it looks, and I'm damned if I'll pay for his burying."

Ed stared at the man, too shocked to grasp at once the full implication of his words. "Dying? What's the matter with him?"

The clerk tapped his chest. "He's got it bad. A storm caught him when he was crossing Blue Mesa. He was burning up with fever when he got here." The clerk paused, and then added, his eyes on Ed: "The doc ain't been paid, neither. If you're any kin of Morgan. . . ."

"You'll get paid," Ed said hotly. "So will the doc. Where is Ben?"

"Room Twelve. Turn left at the head of the stairs."

Ed swung away from the desk and took the stairs three at a time. Dying! Not Ben Morgan who should have most of his life before him, Ben who had paid many times for whatever he had done that was wrong. A man shouldn't have to die because of one mistake. Ben deserved another chance. He had a lot of good in him. He'd just got started wrong.

He found the room and, opening the door, called: "Ben?"

The room was dark, and the air was heavy with the stench of sickness. Ed heard the springs squeak and Ben's weary voice: "Ed, you old horse thief. I knew you'd come."

Ed struck a match and, in the brief light, glimpsed a lamp on the bureau. He lighted it and turned. He stood there, blinking, struggling desperately to hide his emotion as he looked at his brother. A shadow of the Ben he had known. No more than that. White skin pulled tightly across the bones of his long face, red hair a tousled mass, eyes feverishly bright. Ed walked toward the bed, trying to smile and failing. The clerk was right. Death was not far away for Ben Morgan.

"Your letter was slow getting through," Ed said. "I was afraid you'd ridden on, figuring I wasn't coming."

"I won't be riding nowhere except to the boneyard." Ben held out a claw-like hand. "But you got here in time. That's what counts."

Ed gripped his hand, trying to grin. "Sure, boy. I'll get the doc up here. You need rest and good grub. You'll be back on your feet. . . ."

"I never knew you to lie to me before." Ben closed his eyes. "It's no use, Ed. Four years of hell was too much. Took the vinegar out of me. Pull up a chair. I've got some talking to do and not much time."

Ed brought a rawhide-bottom chair to the bed and sat down. No, there was little use in lying to Ben. He knew now he had no worry about what to say, no worry about how to meet the change that had come to Ben. All he had to do was listen.

A coughing spell struck Ben. He held a rag to his mouth, and, when he was quiet, he drew it away, leaving a scarlet froth clinging to his lips. For a moment he was silent, feverish eyes on Ed, as if he could not satisfy the hunger he had for the sight of his brother.

Ed didn't say anything. He couldn't. He just sat there, looking at Ben, his throat swelling so that it was an effort to swallow. He could not believe this was Ben, Ben who had al-

11

ways been wild and strong and a little crazy, doing one risky thing after another that no one else would even have thought of trying.

"Been a long time," Ben said in his weary voice. "Six years. Your letter didn't tell much. You wrote about getting married and losing your wife."

Ed nodded. "Last year. The baby died, too."

"Did you love her, Ed? I mean, really love her, or was she just a woman to sleep with?"

For a moment Ed didn't answer, his gaze fixed on the wall above Ben's bed. He didn't want to talk about it. Finding and marrying Ruth was the finest thing that had ever happened to him. They had lived together one year, one good year out of Ed's twenty-seven; then he had lost her, and the light had gone out for Ed Morgan. But he couldn't tell Ben this, not with Ben dying.

"Yes, I loved her," Ed said, and let it go at that.

A smile touched Ben's lips as if that made it easier. He asked: "So much in love that every thought you had was for her?"

Ed nodded. "That's the way it was."

"She was a good woman, wasn't she? You'd pick that kind."

Ed nodded again. He slumped wearily in his chair, thinking of the year he'd had with Ruth, of the plans they'd made, and how much she had loved the Triangle M. A good woman! She was that and more, so much more that he could not put it into words, and he wouldn't try. Maybe she had been too good to live in Ed's world, a world of hard work and heartbreak and violence, a world in which trouble always outweighed happiness. It was a crazy thought, this notion that she had been too good to live, but he had never understood why she'd had to die. Other women had babies and lived, and

12

their goodness and badness had nothing to do with it.

Ed bowed his head, sick now with the burden of memories that crowded through him. That was the way it always went when he let himself think about it, and he could not help thinking about it now, but Ben did not realize what his questions had done to Ed. He was coughing again, his thin body wrenched by the violence of it. When he was done, he turned his head on the pillow to look at Ed.

"Getting married changed you," Ben said. "I ain't sure just how, but I can feel it. Maybe you ain't so pious. Maybe it softened you so you could have a little fun with your sinning."

Ed raised his head and met Ben's gaze. "No, it didn't soften me, but you're right about me having a little fun with my sinning. I finally figured out this is a god-damned rotten world."

"You're wrong, Ed," Ben said. "I'm the one who ought to think that, but I don't. A man should be thankful for whatever he had that was good. My trouble was that I had to pick out a bitch. I had her for a little while, Ed, and it was fine. She's purty, but that ain't what you think about when you're with her. I didn't think of it when I was in stony lonesome, neither. I couldn't think of anything but the nights I'd slept with her and how good it was."

Ben's big-knuckled hands lay palm down on the blanket, his eyes closed as if thinking of her again, a faint smiling working at the corners of his mouth. "Her name's Honey Travers. She's probably at Gateway House, or will be, if you wait for her. When you see her, you'll know how it was. She turns a man inside out, and she'd do it to you, but I ain't blaming her. She can't help it." He raised a hand to point at his coat, hanging from a nail in the wall. "Get me a piece of paper that's in the pocket."

Ed rose and crossed the room to the coat. Ben had said: "A

13

man ought to be thankful for what he had that was good."
That was surprising coming from Ben, who had never been
thankful for anything when he was a boy. The same thought
had often occurred to Ed, but he had never been able to accept it any more than he'd been able to accept the justice of a
God who had given Ruth to him and then had taken her away.
He found the paper in a side pocket of Ben's coat and brought
it to the bed, a single sheet that had been folded twice.

"Look at it," Ben said. "I drew it before I left Canon City
just on the chance I wouldn't last, but I've kept alive long
enough for you to get here. I don't care now one way or the
other. I know you'll take care of Honey."

Unfolding the paper, Ed saw that a crude map had been
drawn in pencil. The lines were smudged, but after a moment's study Ed could make out the writing **Gateway House**
and **Diablo River** on a wavy line that ran east and west. The
curlicues on the eastern side of the map would represent
mountains. South of the river there was a cross between what
was apparently two pine trees, but a heavy line below the
trees puzzled Ed. The space between the cross and the river
was marked **Jansen Mesa**.

"The line beside the cross is a chunk of rimrock," Ben explained. "Red with streaks of yellow in it. You can't miss it, if
you go due south of the falls. You'll have to locate the falls
from the south rim of Diablo Cañon. You can't get down to
it."

"What's the cross?"

"Fifty thousand dollars," Ben said. "I held up the Casino
in Sentinel and got that far with it before my horse threw a
shoe. I buried the *dinero* between them trees and lit out on
foot. The posse nailed me about a mile from there."

Ben began to cough again. Ed stared at the map, sensing
what was coming and not liking it. Marriage may have

14

changed him, but not so much that he was capable of going after stolen money and giving it to a girl Ben had called a bitch.

When Ben was quiet, he pinned his feverish eyes on Ed, frowning. "Don't get righteous now. That *dinero*'s mine. The gent who owed the Casino was a crook named Vance. I've always been lucky at poker. At least, they say I'm lucky. I figured I was good."

Ed nodded. That was something else he remembered. Ben had always argued that a man was stupid who worked if he could take it away from the other fellow, and the clincher to his argument was that Ben could do it, even when he was a kid.

"I had some luck in Grand Junction," Ben went on. "Some more in Montrose. Then I hit Gateway House and had some more. I took ten thousand off a gent named Dal Barger. He owns Fishhook, a big spread on Jansen Mesa. I went on up to Sentinel with Honey, and I pokered my stake up to fifty thousand. It was crazy luck that hits a man once in a lifetime, but I wasn't smart enough to quit. Vance got me with some crooked dealing and broke me."

"How do you know it was crooked dealing?"

"I spotted it the next night when he was playing with Barger. Barger had followed me up there to get his *dinero* back, but Vance had it by the time Barger got to Sentinel. I hollered about the dealing, then I got slugged and throwed into the alley. When I came to, I was in Barger's hotel room. Honey was there, too."

Ben stopped, too tired to go on. He lay on his back, his eyes closed, barely breathing. Ed, watching him, smoked a cigarette down to a stub and rolled another, and all the time he was thinking that he'd have no part of this, that, as soon as Ben was buried, he'd head back to the Laramie.

"Barger said Vance admitted to him he'd been dealing crooked the night before," Ben said finally, "so Barger said I was entitled to my money, but the only way to get it was to hold up the Casino. He'd see to it I had a relay of fresh horses along the river. I pulled it, got a good haul of gold and greenbacks, just about what I'd lost, and I made it down the San Miguel and over the divide to the Diablo. I grabbed another horse there and got plumb down to the south end of Jansen Mesa when they nabbed me."

"But the money belongs to Vance, even if. . . ."

"He's dead. Honey visited me several times at the pen and told me. She tried to get it out of me where I hid the money, saying she'd hire a good lawyer and I'd be out of the pen in a week, but I wouldn't tell her. She likes money, Ed, money and men. I figured, after I got out, I'd have her again if I could find the *dinero*."

Ben's letter had not even hinted at this. Ed put the map into his pocket, not looking at his brother. He said: "Nothing I can do."

"You can find the dinero," Ben said. "It's mine. Give half of it to Honey and keep the other half. She knows I was coming to Gateway House, so chances are she'll be there. You pretend you're me. Sign my name to the register. We look enough alike for you to make a go of it."

"I don't want it," Ed said. "Let it stay there."

"No. When I was in the pen, I thought about the ranch and how hard you used to work and how damned ornery I was. And I thought about how you could build the spread up with that money. I was going back after I got it. I'd had enough helling around. I was aiming to take Honey with me. Now I want you to take care of her."

"I don't want it," Ed said again. "I don't want your woman, either."

Ben's bony hands were clenched on the blankets. He said: "I never asked anything of you before, Ed, and I wouldn't ask this if I wasn't cashing in. There's just the two of us. I've been wanting to do something for you to kind of balance up for what you tried to do for me. Now it's too late to do anything but this."

Ed rose and walked to the window. He stared into the darkness, remembering how it had been. He'd been a man at eighteen when their father had died; he'd had to be a man because there wasn't anyone else. He did not remember their mother, who had died when he and Ben had been small. Just the three of them: their father and Ed and Ben who resented being bossed by an older brother.

He remembered the bitterness he'd felt when Ben had left the Triangle M. To him, right was right and wrong was wrong, and there was no middle ground. When he'd received Ben's first letter, saying he was in prison, Ed had told himself that was what he'd expected all the time. But he'd been wrong, all wrong. Ruth, who knew nothing about it except what he had told her, had made him see how wrong he'd been, how harsh his judgments had been.

"That *dinero* belongs to him that gets it," Ben said in his tired voice. "I want Honey to have part of it. It's the best I can do for her. You tell her I never stopped loving her. Will you do that, Ed?"

Ed made a slow turn from the window. "You said she was a bitch."

"Does it make any difference? I love her. I keep telling you that. When you see her, you'll want her."

"No, I won't," Ed said, "but that isn't important. I guess your loving her is."

"Then go after the *dinero*. Sign my name like I told you.

17

When Honey finds you, you'll know she loved me."

That made no sense to Ed at the time. He walked back to the bed, realizing suddenly that Ben had very little time left. His eyes were bright and staring; each breath was an effort. He had talked too much, and his strength was gone. Somehow he had held onto life waiting for Ed to come, waiting to tell him about this, and now it was done.

"Will you do it, Ed?" Ben whispered.

"Yes, I'll do it," Ed said. It was the only thing he could say.

Ben smiled. He said: "Thank you, Ed. Watch out for Dal Barger. He'll take the money away from you if he can."

That was all. He dropped off to sleep, and he never woke again. When the doctor came, he felt Ben's pulse and shook his head. "Nothing I can do," he said. "Nothing anybody can do now. You're his brother?"

"Yes."

"I knew he was waiting for you. It kept him alive, I guess. I don't understand how it could, but I've seen things like this happen before. There's not much any of us understand about death. Well, he won't last till sunup."

The doctor was right. Ben died just before dawn. Ed, sitting beside the bed, wondered at the peaceful expression that had come to Ben's face, Ben whose life had been so turbulent when he'd been home. For some strange reason, prison had brought peace into Ben Morgan's life.

Then Ed remembered the promise he'd made. He'd keep it. He had no choice. He'd find Honey Travers, but he wouldn't want her. He'd hate her, and maybe he'd kill her before he was done.

Ben had lacked the time and strength to tell him all of it. There must have been more, much more, but whatever it was, Ed was sure of one thing. If it had not been for Honey

Travers, Ben would not have gone to prison, and he would not be lying here now, Ben who'd had enough helling around and wanted to come home. Yes, Ed would meet her and he'd hate her as he had never hated any other living person.

# Chapter Two

Before Ed left Montrose, he inquired the way to the Diablo River and Gateway House, thinking there would be no danger so far from where the money was hidden, no need to look for Dal Barger yet. He was a stranger in this country. Ben had been, too, and he had been gone for four years, so it seemed unlikely that anyone would remember him in a town that had the shifting population Montrose did. But before Ed had been on the trail half a day, he realized he was being followed.

He camped on Leopard Creek that night, stopping in the shank end of the afternoon. He watered his horse, staked him out in the knee-high grass beside the stream, and built a fire. He cooked supper, listening for the slightest sound that did not belong here in the wilderness and glancing around now and then as any man would who was camping alone in a strange country.

Only silence. And loneliness. No one went by on the road. The sun was down, and twilight was thickening in the bottom of the cañon when he saw a faint show of dust far down the creek. The rider had been coming from upstream along Leopard Creek, but apparently he had turned off. Presently it was dark, the only light the innumerable stars in the strip of sky between the ridges, and still no one had gone by on the road.

Ed let his fire go out. He wondered if he had imagined he was being followed. He had seen the man behind him shortly after he left Montrose. The distance between them remained the same when he started the long climb to Dallas summit. It was not until Ed made camp that he had lost sight of the fellow. The man was still behind him, or he had circled and

20

gone back down the trail to Montrose. He might have circled, Ed decided, and raised the dust he had seen before dark.

Ed rolled a cigarette and lighted it, cupping the match flame in one hand. Then he remembered that the dust had apparently been raised by a man riding downstream along the creek. So there might have been two of them. If either had ridden by, Ed would have given it little thought, but the fact that both had disappeared worried him.

He pondered this as he smoked, but he could make no sense out of it. The trouble was he didn't know the whole story. There was any number of possibilities. Ben might have talked to someone in prison about the buried money. Or, and this seemed more likely, people in Sentinel and Gateway House and on Jansen Mesa knew what had happened four years ago. If the news of Ben's release from prison had reached this country, it was more than possible that someone, perhaps the rancher, Dal Barger, had placed a man in Montrose to watch for Ben.

Fifty thousand dollars was enough to lure half the toughs on the western slope to Gateway House. But personal danger seemed distant and unreal to Ed. If the man who had followed him all day had been watching Ben in Montrose, he would know that Ben was dead. He would also know that his only chance to get the money would be to let Ed lead him to it.

Ed rubbed out his cigarette, then picked up his saddle and blanket and moved back from the creek a good thirty feet. He lay down, discounting the chance of being attacked. If it did happen, there would be a good deal of searching and banging around in the darkness before his new location was discovered.

For a long time he lay on his back, staring upward through the cottonwood branches at the night sky. The wilderness silence was broken only by some tiny animal scampering through the dry leaves, or a coyote barking from the rim above him. Now, in the serene calm of this loneliness, Ed's mind turned from his own trouble to Ben, and Honey Travers.

From the time he had left Montrose that morning, Ed had been haunted by the memory of Ben's death and the funeral. The full tragedy of Ben's life struck him, the tragedy of a rebellious boy who had left home only to go to prison, and then die within a few days after he was released.

All of it seemed unreal to Ed, a horrible nightmare that might have been dredged up from some deep pocket of his consciousness while he was drunk, or when he was so drugged by fatigue that his sleep had been like that of a dead man. But it was real. The proof of it was the fact that he was on his way to see Honey Travers, instead of heading south toward Laramie.

Ed could understand how a wild and turbulent spirit like Ben's had been broken by four years of hell in the Canon City prison. He could understand how Ben's body had been worn down until it lacked the strength to recover from exposure, but he could not understand the love Ben had had for Honey Travers, a love that had not been diminished up to the moment he had lost consciousness. That love, more than anything else, gave Ed the weird feeling that the minutes he had spent talking to Ben had never really happened.

The nineteen-year-old kid Ed remembered would not have risked his life for any woman. So he had changed, and Honey Travers must have been responsible for the change. Ed thought about her now, wondering what she would be like, his curiosity stirred against his will.

She would be waiting at Gateway House. He considered the mental picture he had formed of her: blonde and sensuous and full-bosomed, the kind of woman who made a man crazy with the want of her. She would be tough, Ed thought, tough and calculating and utterly selfish, and, because she liked men and money, she would be waiting. But what would she do when she learned that Ben would never come for her? And what would Ed say and do when he met her? Maybe he would kill her. She deserved it, if she was responsible for Ben's trouble, and the way Ed saw it, she was entirely to blame. Ben had been young and gullible.

Ed drew his gun and laid it beside him. He did not want to go to sleep. Sleeping men died easily, and the uneasiness that resulted from being followed all day lingered in his mind. But the weariness that gripped him was both emotional and physical, and in the end it could not be denied.

He woke once to find the cañon bathed in moonlight. He sat upright, instinctively reaching for his gun, but he could not see or hear anything that was unnatural to this time and place. He lay down again, thinking he had been dreaming, although he could not remember that he had, and once more dropped off to sleep.

The second time he woke the moon was lost behind a western ridge and the sky was overcast so even the stars were hidden. He groped in the darkness for his gun and found it, uncertain what had wakened him but feeling the chill prickle of fear along his spine. Perhaps he had been dreaming again. Still, the presence of another man and the sound of his movement might have stirred him awake.

*The night must be nearly gone,* he thought. Now the earth seemed so completely swallowed by darkness that he could see absolutely nothing. He decided that he was worrying without reason and started to ease back when he caught the unmistakable sound of movement. At first he had the impression that something heavy was being dragged through the dry leaves, then he realized that a man was crawling toward him, very slowly and carefully, and pausing now and then, perhaps to listen.

Ed's first impulse was to dive sideways, to plunge and scratch and scramble like any fugitive animal, to do anything to get away. But the threatened moment of panic passed. The best thing to do was to remain motionless. He wasn't quite sure where the man was or whether the fellow knew his location. Too, there was a possibility that there were two of them, and he might ram into one while trying to get away from the other.

As he listened, sitting bolt upright with the gun gripped in his right hand, he had the impression that the dragging sound came from both sides of him. Then he heard the ominous click of a gun being cocked, and a moment later there was another to his left. There were two of them! No doubt of it. The one who had followed him from Montrose and the other who had been upstream. Somehow they had got together.

"Don't move, Morgan." The voice was between him and the creek and slightly to his left. "We've got double-barreled shotguns loaded with buckshot. You cut loose on us and you're a dead man. We don't care whether we get you alive or dead. What we want is that map your brother gave you."

Ed's first feeling was one of relief. They must have watched him make camp, and now they were assuming he had bedded down in the same place. But it gave him only a minor advantage. No more. If he spoke, he would give away his position. It would be the same if he made any kind of movement.

Then the thought occurred to him that they wanted him alive, or they would have dry-gulched him before dark. It would have been easy enough, if they had been watching him, and he felt certain that they had. Then he thought he knew why. They weren't sure he had the map. If he had destroyed it, and, if they killed him, no one would ever find the money. He had a hole card and a good one.

"Where the hell are you?" the man asked. "Speak up."

"No sense keeping mum," the other man said. "You can't get away. We're between you and your horse. No use throwing any lead at us, neither. A slug from a six-gun don't stick up very high against buckshot. Let's have that map and we'll drift."

Still he said nothing. These men weren't smart, he thought. They were counting on the darkness to cover them, but it served equally well to cover him. Then the confidence that had been in him a moment before began to die. Dawn was not far away. If it came to a showdown—and he saw no way to avoid it—the advantage would be with them. They would kill him before they took a chance of getting killed, even if it meant losing the fifty thousand.

Very carefully he got to his feet, making no sound at all. A big cottonwood stood not more than ten feet to his left. He couldn't see it, but he thought he remembered its exact location. He had to be right when he moved, or he'd run headlong into the tree and knock himself out.

"He's gone," one of the men said, and swore.

"No he ain't," the other snapped. "His horse is still here."

The sound of their voices gave only a slight clue to their location, not enough to risk a shot. It would be sheer luck if he hit one. The flash of his gun in the darkness would give the other a target, and at this distance the man couldn't miss.

"We'll wait till daylight," the first man said. "You work up the hill, Miller. I'll stay here. We'll get him in a crossfire when he does move."

"We don't want to beef him," the other argued. "All he's

got to do is to throw his damned map down here and we'll leave him alone."

The talk was meant for his ears, lying talk, for once they had the map Ed was a dead man. He fished a silver dollar out of his pocket and tossed it toward them, calling: "There's your map!"—and dived sideways toward the cottonwood.

The act was one of desperation. Time was running out for him. He was standing up, and they were lying flat on the ground. Already a faint hint of dawn was showing in the sky above the eastern ridge. Within a matter of minutes he would be visible to them, but they would have the momentary advantage of being lost against the darkness of the ground.

He had hoped they would open up, but he was disappointed. He gained the cover of the tree trunk, then he heard the thin sound of laughter. The one named Miller said: "We flushed our rabbit, Jake. He ain't going nowhere. Nowhere else, I mean."

And the other: "Fifty thousand dollars. Think of what that'll buy a man. I don't see no sense of taking the map back to Gowdy. He don't need the *dinero* half as bad as we do."

For just a moment, Ed hesitated. They thought they had him cornered. He could head upstream through the timber, and, if he started before it was light enough for them to see him, he might make it. He realized at once that it would be the wrong thing to do. They'd be on his tail within a matter of minutes; they'd have horses, and he'd be on foot. No, he was better off to take his chances right here.

He felt cold sweat break through his skin. He had never killed a man, but he was going to now, and, if he had luck, he'd kill two. The chances were they'd be the first of several. Greed did that to men.

They wouldn't be the first to die. It had begun with Ben. The possibility that he might be the next occurred to him, and then passed out of his mind. He was going to do the unexpected. It would work. It had to. He had learned a long time ago that, if a man expected failure, the odds were he'd have it.

"I'm leaving," Ed called. "If you bastards try to follow me, I'll kill you."

He had cocked his gun as he talked. One of the men said: "Don't be a fool, Morgan. All we want is the map. We'll chase. . . ."

Ed charged directly at the man, yelling: "I told you I was leaving!" Get them thinking one thing, when you're in a pinch, and then do the opposite. A veteran Wyoming lawman had once told him that, and now it seemed to Ed it was the only thing he could do.

He covered half the distance between him and the first man before he fell flat on his stomach. He used several seconds, gambling that it would take that long for the men to realize what he had done. He won his bet. They fired at the same time, powder flame leaping out into the darkness, the explosions close and thunder-loud to Ed's ears, the buckshot flying overhead. He threw a bullet at the closest man, heard the grunt that was jolted out of him, and scrambled frantically toward the creek.

"I'm hit!" the man yelled. "Get him, Miller."

Again a shotgun blasted at Ed, but he was moving fast down the slope toward the stream. He went over the bank in a rolling fall, going into the water before he could stop. But he had held onto his gun, and he had used only one bullet. Now, shocked by the impact of the cold water, he scrambled out of it and fell forward against the dirt of the steep bank.

He had no way of knowing how hard the man was hit. As he lay there, laboring with his breathing, he heard the injured one scream: "Come back here, Miller, or I'll let you have it!" But Miller must have given way to panic, for he came floundering down the slope toward the creek, apparently thinking only of getting away.

The wounded man fired, screaming and cursing at the other for his cowardice. Miller sprawled into the creek within ten feet of where Ed crouched against the bank, sliding into the water in a shower of dirt and gravel. Ed fired at him three times, spreading his shots two feet apart. He held one bullet, staring into the darkness in an effort to locate the man's body, but he could not.

After the echo of gunfire had faded, and the gravel and dirt stopped running down the bank, Ed heard the gurgling sound of the man's breathing, but only for a moment. Then that, too, stopped. Ed crawled to the man, who lay half in the water, and felt his pulse. There wasn't the slightest flicker.

Whether the other man had got him with the buckshot, or whether Ed had killed him, was something he didn't know, and he didn't take time to find out. He started upstream, keeping down so the bank to his right protected him. He intended to get his horse and leave, then he remembered that his saddle was near the wounded man. He'd have to wait.

He pulled himself over the bank into the grass. He lay there, weak and a little sick as he wondered if it was finished, if he had actually killed two men. Presently the wounded man called: "Morgan!" Ed didn't answer. A moment later the man said: "I'm cashing in, Morgan. You got me in the belly. You were lucky, mister, mighty damned lucky."

Ed crawled toward him, then stopped. There was some light now, gray and thin, but enough to make out the vague shape of the ridges and trees and the tall upthrusts of rock beside the creek. The man said: "I hear you, Morgan. You're coming to finish me. All right, you do that, but you're wasting your lead. I'll tell you one thing. Spur Gowdy will get you. You're a dead man."

"How'd you know about the map?"

"I had the room next to your brother's. Heard you talking the night he died. Didn't know he had a map or I'd have got it sooner. Tried to make him tell me where the *dinero* was, but he wouldn't."

The man became silent, no sound coming from him except the steady rasp that was his breathing. Ed thought about him, well and strong, trying to make a dying man say something he didn't want to say, and in that moment he had more admiration for Ben than he'd ever had before in his life.

"You son-of-a-bitch," Ed said. "I'm going to kill you for what you done to Ben."

"You already have," the man said. "You fired one shot, when it was so damned dark you couldn't see nothing, and you hit me. Your brother was just as lucky for a while. He got two of Barger's men after he held up the Casino, but his luck ran out. So will yours."

Ed started crawling toward the man again, thinking that Ben should have told him what to expect, but he'd had too much else to tell and so little time. Back of these men who had attacked Ed was someone named Spur Gowdy, and probably back of him was the rancher, Dal Barger.

Suddenly Ed was aware that the man was not making that rasping sound. He must have stopped breathing. Ed, holding his cocked gun in his right hand, wormed his way through the grass until he reached him. The man was dead.

Ed got his horse and saddled up. A few minutes later he was riding upstream in the direction of the San Miguel River, the sun reaching toward the bottom of the cañon and throwing its scarlet light on the western ridge.

He still had a long ride, for the Diablo was far south of the

San Miguel, and Gateway House was on the Diablo. He was tired, sick and tired, of this business before he had really started, but he had made a promise, and Ben could not release him from it.

# Chapter Three

Darkness overtook Ed before he reached the Diablo. He put his horse down the steep north bank to the water, and let the animal drink. Ed's eyes were on the cluster of lights across the river. From the directions he had been given at Montrose, he judged this was Gateway House, the only stopping place between here and Sentinel.

He watched men move across the lantern-lighted yard; he heard shouts and bits of ribald songs from others in the bar. A typical place of its kind, he thought. High-stake games such as Ben had played here with Dal Barger would not be unusual. Murder would be only a little less unusual. It would be the same with the robbery Ben had committed in Sentinel. As for Honey Travers, she represented a kind of sin that was the most common of all and could be bought either here or in Sentinel by any man who had the money. She wasn't worth it, Ed told himself bitterly. She wasn't worth even a small part of the price Ben Morgan had paid.

A narrow bridge without guardrails of any kind spanned the river a few feet below Ed. Now he heard the sound of boot heels on the plank floor of the bridge, and a man called out: "This is Gateway House, mister. You can get a bed and good grub and all the whisky you can drink."

Ed stepped into the saddle and reined his buckskin back up the bank. He said: "For them that have the money to pay, you mean."

The man laughed. "Hell, mister, you don't figger we're in business 'cause we like the climate, do you?"

"No, I didn't figure that." Ed rode onto the bridge. "You always drum up trade this way?"

"Why not? Lots of fellers don't know what we've got here,

31

so they start upstream, expecting to find a town. It's a long ride to Sentinel, friend."

Ed had reached the man by then. In the thin light, he could not make out the fellow's face, but he could see that he was old and stooped. He said: "I'll take your deal, but if the grub ain't good, I'll ask for my money back."

"That's fair." The old man's head was tipped back, his eyes pinned on Ed's face. "Been here before?"

Ed did not know why Ben had asked him to change identity, but he'd play it out because that was the way his brother had wanted it. He said: "Yeah, I was here four years ago."

"You're Morgan, ain't you?"

"That's right."

The old man let out a long breath. "Well, now, we've been expecting you ever since we heard you'd got out of stony lonesome. What held you up?"

"I was sick."

"It's my guess you'll be sicker before you're done. You know, Morgan, a lot of folks have been expecting you. But that's your business, not mine. You don't remember me, I reckon. I'm Billy Lowe. I work for Grace Doane. You'll recollect her, though she was some younger the last time you was here. Her pa was running the place then."

"Sure, I remember her."

"Well, come along. Grace will see you get fed, even if the dining room is closed. She's that way. She'll get up in the middle of the night to feed any stray that drifts in."

They crossed the bridge, Lowe keeping up with the buckskin. When they reached the south side of the river, the old man said: "Put your animal in yonder barn. Hamp will rub him down and feed him. Good man with horses, Hamp is."

Lowe swung toward the house and crossed the yard in a half run. So a lot of folks were expecting Ben Morgan. Not that there was anything surprising about people expecting his brother. A couple of dead men on Leopard Creek proved that point. But it was surprising that Billy Lowe would say it in so many words, and it was even more surprising that he'd say: "We've been expecting you." Who was the *we?* Well, Ed would find out before long.

He rode into the barn and dismounted. A man shuffled out of a back stall, calling: "I'll take your horse, mister! Better get into the house and see if there's any grub left. Got a crowd tonight. Hell of a big crowd."

Ed cuffed back his hat so that a stray lock of red hair showed along his forehead. "You're Hamp?"

This man was as old and stooped as Billy Lowe. He bobbed his head, stroking his wisp of a beard. "I'm Hamp. Been taking care of horses at Gateway House for years." He chewed a liver-colored lip, frowning thoughtfully. "See you're that Morgan *hombre,* ain't you?"

Ed had been uneasy from the first about taking Ben's identity, and now the uneasiness grew. One man had heard the truth through the paper-thin wall of the hotel in Montrose. He was dead, but had he told anyone? And how well had these people known Ben and how long had he stayed here? Ed couldn't pull it off, he thought desperately, having learned as little as he had from Ben. He wouldn't even recognize Honey Travers, and she'd know with the first look she gave him that he wasn't Ben. But he had to try.

"Yeah, I'm Morgan," Ed said, "but I don't remember you. Been four years, you know."

Hamp stroked a lean nose. "Four damned long years, mister, with that bastard of a Dal Barger squeezing like he is. But I've seen some long years in my time. Worked for Grace's Daddy when he built the first Gateway House just after they made the strike up the Diablo, but you know, Morgan, in all this time nothing happened that was any bigger than that game you had with Barger. That makes you a big man in these parts. Nobody's gonna forget the *hombre* who took ten thousand off Barger. No, sir."

Ed stripped gear from his buckskin. Picking up his war sack, he said: "Double feeding of oats."

"Sure, sure," Hamp said. "I know how to take care of a horse that's been ridden like this animal has."

Ed swung toward the archway. For an instant he was directly under the lantern that swung from a nail overhead, and in that instant a small hand reached out of the shadows and, gripping his arm, tugged at it. A woman said: "You damned fool. Get out of the light."

He obeyed, thinking this would be Honey Travers. She led him along the wide front of the barn. She stopped at the corner and looked up at him, her face a round blob in the starlight. She said in disgust: "You are a fool, Morgan, taking crazy chances like you always did. You didn't learn anything in prison, did you?"

This wasn't Honey Travers. Ed didn't know why he was so sure, but there wasn't the slightest doubt in his mind. He said: "I'm not smart. That it?"

"That's it. You're not even high-class stupid. If you thought Dal Barger's given up, you're crazier than I thought you were. Spur Gowdy's here."

So he had guessed right. Barger was back of Gowdy. He said: "What's Gowdy doing here?"

"What's the matter with you?" she asked. "You think Honey wouldn't tell Barger you were coming?"

"No, I didn't think she would."

"You mean you hoped she wouldn't," the woman jeered. "I don't understand you, Morgan. I never did. I just can't savvy how a man who's smart in some ways can be such a fool when it comes to Honey Travers. She's been keeping house for Barger ever since they sent you up. She says she's his housekeeper, but I've got another name for it."

"Barger's not here?"

"Prison must have made you a little daft. Or ruined your memory. You know Barger never gets his hands dirty on a job Gowdy can do. If they get their hands on you, they'll get what they want out of you. That's why I've had Billy watching for you ever since I heard you were getting out."

"I'm obliged," Ed said.

"You ought to be. Maybe gratitude's something you learned. Come on. We'll go in through the back."

She darted across a patch of light and was lost behind a shed. When Ed caught up with her, she took his hand. "I'll lead you, or you'll bark your shin and let out a holler. Then they'll be on you like a pack of wolves."

She led him through an aspen clump, making a wide circle toward the back of the house so that the lights were lost for a time. Suddenly she stopped and faced him, her hand still gripping him. It was a soft, warm hand, and she stood close to him, so close that he could feel the pressure of her breasts, and he could hear her breathing. He still had no idea who she was, or what her relationship to Ben had been.

"Morgan, I loaned you a horse," she said. "I'm thinking you need your memory jogged. What you don't know is that I had a hell of a time explaining to the sheriff how you got hold of my black gelding. If he found out I was helping you now, I'd be in trouble."

"You don't have to," he said sharply.

"Oh, yes, I do. Or is your memory so bad you forget the deal we made?"

He had no idea what the deal was, or even whether there had been one. Ben should have told him about this woman, but Ben hadn't been able to think of anyone but Honey Travers. Now Ed could do nothing but play it out and hope he didn't say the wrong thing. "I'd like to forget that deal," he said.

"I'll bet you would," she snapped, "but I won't let you. I aim to have my part of that money, so I'll help you find it. You'll need fresh horses and grub. I'll see that you get anything you need."

She went on, still holding his hand, and presently he could make out the sprawling shape of the big house, the rear wall of it dark except for a single light directly in front of them.

"I don't think Gowdy has any notion you're here," she said, "but we'll make a run for it anyhow. Gowdy's got a brain like a coyote."

They raced across the open space toward the lighted window; she opened a door and went in, pulling him in after her. She closed it quickly and leaned against it, panting. She said: "You're safe for a while. You can thank me when you get around to it."

"Yeah, thanks."

They were in a bedroom, a woman's bedroom, probably hers. He glanced around at the marble-topped bureau, the rocking chair, the bed with the white lace coverlet. He made a slow turn to face the woman. Suddenly, as if only then aware that the shade was still up, she took two long steps toward the window and pulled the green shade down. She turned to Ed and stopped, motionless, apprehension flowing across her face.

She was a small woman, somewhere in her early twenties, with auburn hair that seemed almost red in the lamplight. Her dark brown eyes were fixed on his face with brittle intensity. She wasn't pretty, he decided, not the way some women were with a perfection of features that brought men's eyes to

36

them. Her mouth was too long, her nose too short, her angular cheek bones high on the sides of her face.

Now, meeting her gaze, it struck him that she was not a woman to place a high value upon her appearance. He sensed something about her that was hard to define, an independence of spirit, perhaps, a directness that was almost manlike. For a moment their eyes locked, each coolly appraising the other, and it was Ed who looked away.

"I'll fix you something to eat," she said, and taking the lamp from the bureau, opened a door and stepped into a small kitchen. "I cook some of my own meals when I get too tired of running this crazy place. I have my moments of weakness when I think I'll let Barger have Gateway House for what he'll give. I can't fight him forever."

Ed followed her into the kitchen and sat down at the table. He rolled a smoke, watching her stoke up the fire with pieces of aspen, move the coffee pot to the front of the stove, and set a table for him. She moved with such quick, fluid movements, stopping once to listen, as if conscious of some outside danger, then stepped into the bedroom and dropped a bar across the door. She must be, Ed thought, the Grace Doane that Billy Lowe had mentioned.

She returned to the kitchen and brought biscuits, cold meat, and a slab of peach pie from the pantry. She poured his coffee, and dropped into a chair across the table from him. Putting her elbows on the table, she laced her fingers together and lowered her chin to them.

"Now you can talk, mister," she said. "Just who in the hell are you?"

He looked up from his plate, startled. "Morgan. You called me that. I thought you knew."

"Do I look like I was born this morning? Look, mister, I'm no knucklehead. I knew Ben Morgan pretty well. Not the way

Honey Travers knew him, but I knew him, and you're not him."

"It's been four years."

"Sure, sure, but I've got a good memory. You're built long and lanky like him, and you've got his red hair. You've got the same wide chin with a dimple in it, and you've even got freckles on your nose like he had, but you're not Ben and don't tell me you are. Now what's your game?"

He drank his coffee, staring over the top of his cup at her. This wasn't going the way he had hoped it would. He hadn't seen Honey Travers, and he had a hunch this Doane girl would keep him from seeing her if she could. He put his cup down, the uneasiness in him again. He knew nothing about her; he had no assurance he could trust her.

"How do you know I'm not Ben?" he asked finally.

She straightened, making a quick, impatient gesture that was characteristic of her. "You were mighty vague about some things Ben would have remembered. Besides, you don't look like a man who just got out of prison. You aren't smart, or you'd have thought of that."

"You said once before I wasn't smart."

She laughed. "I'm saying it again. And there's another thing. Ben wasn't one to come in through the back door. Not that he's against coming into a woman's bedroom, but he'd have hunted Gowdy up first. Anyhow, he knew how far he'd get in my bedroom."

"You thought I was Ben when you yanked me out of the light in front of the barn. If you're so smart, why didn't you know I wasn't Ben then?"

"I hadn't got a good look at you, and Billy Lowe told me Ben was out here. Anyhow, I've seen prison change men. It might have changed him."

"All right. It changed me."

"Oh, hell! You haven't been in prison. Now let's quit playing games. Who are you?"

He grinned at her. "You can call me Jones."

She got up, and filled his coffee cup. "Mister, I wasn't fooling about Barger and Gowdy. Since you're calling yourself Morgan, I'm guessing you know where the money is. Maybe Ben told you and kept on riding, afraid to come back here, although that doesn't sound like him. Or maybe you tricked him into telling you where it was, and you killed him. Well, it doesn't make any difference as far as you're concerned. Dal Barger will think you know where the money is, and he'll work you over till you tell him how to find it."

"All right," Ed said. "I know where it is."

She stood looking down at him, color working into her cheeks. She said in a low tone: "That's fine, friend, real fine. Now I'll tell you just what that deal was. When Ben rode in here with a posse on his tail, I gave him my black gelding. He promised I'd get half of the money. Now you're needing help. Are you going to keep Ben's promise?"

He shook his head. "I ain't beholden on account of any promise he made."

She sat down, her clenched fists on the table top, her face dark with suppressed fury. "Looks like I'd better go get Gowdy," she said savagely.

He went on eating, saying nothing. The girl's mouth had formed a hard, bitter line across her face. He glanced at her, feeling her anger, and lowered his eyes to his plate, certain now of one thing. Grace Doane was not a woman he could trust. He had made a mistake telling her he knew where the money was.

"Honey here?" Ed asked.

"Not just this minute, but she'll be along. She's been renting a room for Ben for a week now. It's real handy to hers.

That's the thing she'd think about. You know what she'll do when she finds out you're not Ben? She'll turn you over to Gowdy, after she makes some purty promises, and Barger's boys will bust you up. She'll laugh while they do it, too."

He finished his meal and stood up, deciding he didn't like Grace Doane. He said: "I want to see Honey."

"She's out riding. I'll take you up to the room she rented for Ben, if you're bound to see her, but don't tell her anything. I'm the one who can help you. Don't you forget it."

"You've got a register, haven't you?"

She had moved to the door that led into the front of the house. Now she whirled back to face him, frowning as she raised a hand to brush back a stray lock of auburn hair. "I've waited four years to collect on the promise Ben made me. If I help you, I'll have a bigger investment in this business than I had before. Are you going to give me my share or not?"

"I don't know. Anyhow, I want to sign your register."

"No reason to sign it."

"There is a reason which is my business."

"It'll be better if your name isn't on that register."

"I want it there," he said doggedly, "and I'll see that it's there. You savvy that?"

She flounced back toward the door, calling over her shoulder: "Come on. I can't keep you from being a fool, if you've got to be one."

She led him down a narrow hall that was thinly lighted by a bracket lamp, and went on into the lobby. She flung out a hand toward the crude desk. "You can register now, Mister Jones."

Ed paused in the doorway, wary eyes sweeping the room. A man sat in the far corner, a newspaper in front of his face. No one else was here. Racket flowed in through an open door from the bar: the tinkle of glasses, laughter, and the heavy sound of men talking, with now and then a burst of song. Gateway House was typical of many trailside places Ed had seen, even to the lobby with its rough pine desk, the rawhide-bottom chairs, the stairs that led to the rooms above, and the barren log walls with their gray mud chinking.

The man in the chair was motionless. Smoke lifted from his cigar and floated across the room in shifting blue waves. He gave no sign that he knew anyone had come in. Ed moved to the desk, keeping the man within range of his vision. He dipped the pen in ink and wrote: **Ben Morgan, Canon City, Colorado**. He backed toward the stairs, still watching the man.

Grace Doane had stepped behind the desk, a clenched fist on the pine surface, the other at her side. She said: "Go on up, Mister Jones."

Ed was on the third step when the man in the chair dropped his paper and rose. He said: "Wait, friend. I'm always curious about gents who call themselves Jones."

The lamp behind the desk threw yellow light across the lobby. Ed, his lean body tense, watched the man move to the desk. When he was still two steps from Grace Doane, she lifted a cocked gun from her side. "Stop right there, Gowdy," she said. "Why are you interested in men who call themselves Jones?"

"Why, I get to wondering what their first names are," he said, and lifted his head to pin speculative eyes on Ed. "Worries me so I can't sleep at night."

He was about thirty, Ed judged, a medium-tall, slight man with a round, bland face that might have belonged to any transient drummer. His fixed smile was meaningless, his manner casual, as if he were prompted by nothing more than mild curiosity. His eyes, Ed saw, were pale blue. Long-fingered hands hung at his sides, right hand slightly higher than his left and quite close to the butt of his holstered .45.

Grace said: "Go on upstairs, Mister Jones."

"I'm not real sleepy yet," Ed said.

Gowdy's guileless eyes dropped to Grace's tense face. "You're right handy with that popgun, ma'am. Someday you're gonna pull it on the wrong man."

"Not if that man's you," she said.

Ignoring the gun and her warning, he took two long steps to the register and spun it around. Grace moved back so that he could not reach her across the desk, the gun still on him. Again Gowdy lifted his head to look at Ed, the fixed smile unchanged. He said: "How were things in Canon City, Mister Jones?"

"Fine," Ed said, "except that they're waiting for you."

For an instant Ed thought he had prodded Gowdy too far, that any prodding would have been too much. The smile had been wiped from the gunman's lips. Ed had never seen a more innocuous-looking man in his life, but he realized this was a pose, that Spur Gowdy was thoroughly dangerous.

If it came to the shooting stage, Ed's gun would still be in his holster when Gowdy's went into action. Then he saw a grin break across Gowdy's face, and he knew nothing would come of this now. Perhaps Gowdy was wondering what had happened to his men who were supposed to be watching for Ben Morgan.

"I aim to keep the Canon City folks waiting a little longer," Gowdy said easily. He backed away, left hand coming up in a gesture of mock farewell. "Have a good sleep, Mister Jones." He turned and strode into the bar.

Grace replaced the gun under the desk. Picking up a key from the board on the wall, she glared at Ed, her breasts rising and falling with the fury that possessed her. She said bitterly: "So you wouldn't let me hide you. You just had to let them know you were here and that you're pretending to be Ben Morgan. Well, maybe you don't know that Gowdy is the fastest man on the Diablo."

"I figured he was," Ed said. "Who do you mean by *them?*"

"Gowdy and Barger. You know whom I meant. Or are you so stupid you don't know what you're up against?"

"The way you tell it, it doesn't seem to make much difference what I'm up against. Honey would tell Barger I'm here, wouldn't she?"

"Maybe not. There's one thing you can count on from Honey. She'll take the best offer she gets. You'll know that before morning." Grace flounced around the desk. "I'll show you Ben's room. I mean, the room Honey rented for him. She may put a knife in your ribs, when she finds out you're fooling her, but they're your ribs. I'm not going to worry about them."

No, she wouldn't, Ed thought as they went up the stairs. Grace Doane wasn't worrying about anything except her share of the fifty thousand dollars.

# Chapter Four

When they reached the head of the stairs, Grace said: "Turn left." Ed swung that way, Grace catching up with him and moving ahead so that she reached a door at the end of the hall before he did. She unlocked the door and, opening it, went in. She struck a match and lighted the lamp on the bureau.

"I had Billy fetch your war sack up," she said. "I'll get it."

She left the room and was back a moment later with the war sack. She dropped it beside the bed and motioned to a door on the other side of the room. "That door opens onto a gallery. Honey has the room on the east side, and the room on the west side is vacated. There's just the three rooms that face the gallery. Nobody will bother you tonight but Honey." She pinned truculent eyes on him. "If you don't want to be bothered by her, I can give you another room."

"This room will do." Ed took off his Stetson and laid it on the bureau. "I get the notion you don't like Honey."

"You get the right notion." She put her hands on her slim hips, her small body tense and defiant. "Look, Red. It doesn't make a damned bit of difference to me whether you think I'm a liar or not, and I don't care what you and Honey do. The only thing I'm interested in is getting half that money Ben Morgan hid, and I've got a right to it."

"A lot of people seem to be interested in that *dinero*."

"Fifty thousand is enough to interest a lot of people, including Dal Barger."

"If Barger wants it, he wouldn't kill me."

"Don't count on that, not if he thinks you're Ben or anybody else who's going to run off with Honey Travers. I'd hate to bet which he wants the most, the woman or the money."

Ed rolled a smoke and sealed it, his eyes on the girl's taut,

44

pale face. "What kind of a gent is this Barger?"

She laughed shortly. "He's not like any man you ever met. If you live on the Miguel or the Diablo or out on Jansen Mesa, you're never free from his shadow. It's all around you, sometimes even blotting out the sun."

Ed stood with his back to the lamp. Grace had moved to the door and put a hand on the knob. Now she turned her head to watch him thumb a match to life and light his cigarette, the flame throwing its momentary light across his dark, lean face. He blew it out, waiting for her to go, but she wasn't ready yet. He said: "Well?"

"Isn't this a hell of a life?" she said with a sudden rush of bitterness. "I want to get off the Diablo with enough money to buy another hotel so I can be free of Dal Barger. This is the only chance I ever had, but you won't let me have it."

"How do you know I won't?"

"Because you'll have a big night, mister, a real big night, and after that you'll never be free of Honey. It was that way with Ben. She's got a way of making you crazy." Grace opened the door, but still she stood there as if wanting something she knew was beyond her reach. Then she said: "I'll help you, if you'll let me. Try to remember that."

She went out then, and, when her steps died along the hall, he locked the door. He blew out the lamp, then crossed the dark room, opened the gallery door, and stepped through it. Most of the lamps in Gateway House were out now except for those in the bar and lobby, and on across the yard the lantern hanging in the archway of the barn made a small, murky hole in the mountain darkness.

A man crossed the yard from the house to the barn, and, as he moved through the archway, Ed saw that it was Spur Gowdy. The man shouted—"Hamp!"—and went inside. A moment later he rode out of the barn, swung around it, and was swallowed by the night. Presently the sound of his passage was gone.

Minutes slid by. The racket coming from the bar below Ed died; the lamps winked out. The only sounds in the night were the whisper of wind in the aspens and the liquid laughter of the river as it rushed by. The moonlight thinned the darkness, and ridge lines on both sides of Gateway House seemed to press against it, long, black lines that melted vaguely into the star-speckled sky.

Now, with time to think about what had happened from the moment he had left Montrose, Ed tried to make a pattern out of it, but only one fact was clear. Many people expected to have all or part of the hidden money. Grace Doane made no secret of her hunger for it, but Ed was bound by Ben's wishes, Ben who had loved Honey Travers and wanted her to have her share of the money. Either he had forgotten his deal with Grace, or he hadn't cared. Or Grace might be lying.

Fifty thousand dollars, greenbacks and gold, it was found money that belonged to no one, or so Ben had told it. Ed could do a great deal with fifty thousand. It was more than he would make in a lifetime struggling with his shirt tail spread on the upper Laramie. Honey did not deserve any of it, not if she belonged to Barger.

The prospect of taking all the money grew on Ed. He could make the Triangle M into the kind of spread that he and Ruth had dreamed about. Ruth was in his mind then, filling it completely. He let himself think of the good months they'd had together, of their plans and the bright hope of a son. But the months were only a memory, a brief, false promise, and with Ruth's death had gone Ed Morgan's gift for laughter.

An empty loneliness clawed through Ed, a loneliness that had grown in intensity since he had watched Ben die. He realized now how much he had counted on Ben's return, even though he had consciously tried to keep the idea out of his mind because he'd had no reason to expect it. Still, it had been there.

A coyote barked from the ridge to the south, a haunting cry that made Ed lift his head to stare into the darkness. The sound came out of the wilderness; it belonged to the wilderness, and it expressed Ed's feelings as he could not express them himself. He felt a kinship of spirit with the coyote that was up there somewhere in the spruce, giving voice to his loneliness, calling for something he needed and perhaps did not fully understand himself. But there was no answer; there was never any answer to loneliness.

Ed thought of Grace's saying: "Isn't this a hell of a life?" He had said the same thing to himself. He had every reason to say it. He'd had his months with Ruth, and then she was gone, and it would have been better if he'd never had her. There was no fairness or decency or justice in life, or it wouldn't have gone that way.

Now, drained of emotion, he thought again of what he could do for the Triangle M with fifty thousand dollars. Plenty of unused range on the upper Laramie. He could have a big herd. Good cattle. A dozen cowhands to fight the bad weather, when it came, while he stayed inside and kept warm. If a man had ambition and pride, he grew until he was so big that his shadow darkened an entire range, just as Dal Barger's shadow was covering this country. Big money could do that, and fifty thousand was big.

Ed went inside and pulled off his boots, tired of waiting. Grace had said Honey would be along tonight. Well, he'd get rid of her. He didn't owe her a damned thing. Let her live with Dal Barger, if that was the kind of life she wanted. It should satisfy her.

He dropped off into a troubled sleep, waking once with the vague impression that a horse had been ridden into the yard below him. He went to sleep again, not sure whether he had dreamed it or not. Then he woke again, startled by the knowledge that someone was in the room with him.

A woman had come in through the gallery door. She called softly: "Ben."

He waited, saying nothing, watching her cross the room to his bed, the moonlight upon her. Even now he could not be sure this was real, for in the past he had dreamed Ruth was alive and coming to him at night, but when he'd reached for her, he'd found there was no substance to her, and then he'd been fully awake and deeply troubled by the knowledge that he was still alone.

But he wasn't dreaming now. The woman sat down on the side of the bed and bent over him. His throat was dry. No sound came out of him. Excitement hit him like an electric current. He could not see her face clearly, but he knew exactly what Ben had meant when he'd said: "She turns a man inside out."

He heard her murmur: "Ben, Ben, wake up."

Her lips came down to his, full, rich lips that were hot with passion, crushing his with wanton savagery. Suddenly he seemed to hear Ben shouting at him: *You're not being fair, Ed! She thinks it's me!*

He pushed her back, saying thickly: "I'm not Ben. I'm his brother, Ed."

She smothered a scream and slid away from him. She fell off the bed in a frantic effort to get away. He heard her hit the floor so hard that the pitcher clattered with startling loudness against the top of the bureau. She jumped up and lunged toward the gallery door, but he was there ahead of her, cutting off her retreat.

48

"You're Honey Travers, aren't you?" he asked. "If you are, I want to talk to you."

She said nothing for a long moment. She retreated until she stood against the hall door, and he heard her breathing, an aching, labored sound. Suddenly she cried: "Why did you do a thing like this?"

"I'll light a lamp," he said. "Then we'll talk."

He fished a match out of his shirt pocket, not yet certain whether she would stay. He moved to the bureau and struck the match. He lifted the chimney and touched the flame to the wick and slipped the chimney back into place, his eyes on her. He had expected her to make another run for the gallery door, but she stood motionless, one hand clutching her throat, her frightened eyes searching his face.

"Where is Ben?" she whispered.

Now, for some reason, he found it hard to talk. He stared at her, not disappointed in what he saw but completely surprised. She was younger than he had expected, and she was attractive, a sweet-faced woman with none of the tough, hard-faced appearance of one who had graduated from a bawdy house. Her eyes were blue-green. He could not be sure which color they were. Her hair hung down her back in a smooth yellow mass; her full red lips were parted from white teeth. She was a tall woman, well-proportioned, her black riding skirt pulled tightly against round hips and thighs.

In almost every way she had the physical appearance of the woman he had visualized, yet she was entirely different. It puzzled him, for the difference was an intangible quality of spirit rather than body. Perhaps it was the inherent element of goodness he sensed about her; he'd expected to find a thoroughly selfish and evil woman.

"I didn't think you were like this," she said in an accusing voice. "Ben used to talk about you as if you were kind and decent, but you aren't, or you wouldn't have signed his name to the register."

"He told me to," Ed said.

"You're a liar!" Suddenly she was angry, her face hot and bright with it. She crossed the room to him and slapped him on the cheek, a hard blow that rocked his head and left its sting. "You know what I was to Ben, and you wanted it and then you lost your nerve. You're no good, Morgan."

He stepped back, feeling as guilty as she'd said. "No, I guess I'm not," he admitted.

"If I had a gun, I'd kill you."

She meant it, and then he remembered what Grace Doane had said about her, and that even Ben had not completely trusted her. He said: "If you killed me, you'd never find the money. That's what you want, isn't it?"

"No." She sat down on the edge of the bed, her face pale. "It's Ben I want. Where is he?"

"Dead."

For a moment he thought she was going to faint, and he regretted having said it so bluntly. She swayed, her head bowed, her hands clenched on her lap, then she began to cry softly. It was honest grief, he thought, and he swore at himself for completely misjudging her. Grace Doane was wrong about her. Even Ben had been wrong.

He came to the bed and sat down beside her. "I'm sorry." He put an arm around her, and she leaned against him, and he let her cry. He had no idea of time. He held her that way while the minutes fell behind.

Presently she pushed him away and rose. She looked down at him, hating him, and somehow forced herself to say: "Tell me about it."

"I had a letter, asking me to meet him in Montrose. He was getting out of the pen, and he needed help, but he didn't

50

say what kind of help. The letter was slow getting to me, so I was late. I found him dying. He'd got caught in a storm coming over Blue Mesa, and he had a fever. He died before sunup."

"Was he able to talk?"

Ed nodded. He rose and walked restlessly around the room, asking himself how wrong a man could be. He had condemned her without knowing her, without ever seeing her. Now, looking at her, he saw that her lips were trembling. Tears were running down her cheeks.

"I guess the only reason Ben stayed alive was because he had to talk to me," Ed said. "He told me he loved you."

She rose and gave him her back. He remembered his thoughts, sitting beside Ben's bed: that he'd hate Honey Travers and he'd kill her for what she had done to Ben. But he didn't hate her. Maybe she had not done anything to Ben; maybe he had got into trouble because he had wanted to do something for her. If she had brought even a little happiness to Ben, Ed had no right to blame her for anything.

"He told me where the money's hidden," Ed said. "He wanted you to have some of it."

"That's like Ben, so like him." She sat down on the bed again, her eyes on the floor. "I've known one good man, one good, decent man."

"What happened in Sentinel? After he was knocked out and thrown into the alley?"

She looked up, startled. "He told you about that?"

Ed nodded. "He said he won some money from Barger here in Gateway House, and then he got lucky in the Casino. He lost everything, he said, and after that he caught Vance cheating and he got knocked out."

"What else?"

"He was in a hotel room when he came to. You and Barger were there."

51

"Barger carried him to the room," she said. "If we'd left him in the alley, Vance would have had him murdered, so we hid him until the next night."

"Who had the idea of holding up the Casino?"

"Ben. He couldn't get over losing his money. We'd planned to go back to you. We were going to get married. Ben wanted to settle down."

Ed nodded, a sense of guilt lying heavily upon him. Ben wasn't the only one who had grown up, and now Ed was remembering that Ben had said marriage had changed him. It wouldn't have worked out, if Ben had come home four years ago. Ed knew he wouldn't have been ready, for he was the one who had needed more time.

"From what Ben told me, it seemed to me you two never understood each other," Honey said. "You were eighteen, and he was sixteen when your father died, and you were bound to run the ranch and make Ben do a man's work. He stood it as long as he could, and then he had to get out. It never occurred to you to make him a partner, or that he'd resent being bossed by his older brother."

She was staring at the floor again, her fingers working nervously on her lap. She went on: "After he left home, he drifted down the Grand River. I met him in Grand Junction. He'd learned to handle cards. He made a stake, a few thousand dollars, and we kept moving from one town to another. Then he got lucky in the big game with Barger and that's what started our bad luck."

"He told me Barger promised him a relay of horses. I don't savvy that."

"Barger was sore about losing the money here at Gateway House. Ben promised to return the ten thousand if Barger helped him get away. He was going to Utah, and I was to meet him in Moab."

"Grace Doane said she gave him a horse, and he promised to give her half of the money."

Honey's head snapped up. "She's lying. Anything she tells you is a lie. He paid her for the horse, when he took it. The money was his, all but the ten thousand Barger was to get." She shook her head. "Grace has probably told you a lot of lies about me. She even wrote to Ben, when he was in prison, and I guess he believed her filthy lies."

That explained why Ben had called Honey a bitch, but he could not tell her that, so he said: "He told me he loved you. Don't forget that."

"I never will." She rose and walked toward him. "Ed, I'm going back to the ranch with you. I'm sorry about what I said a while ago, and for hitting you. I guess I was out of my head." She gave him a long, searching look. "I can't stay here. I've been keeping house for Barger, just waiting for Ben. I had to make a living, so I took anything I could get. I'll work for you, Ed, just for a place to live and my food and clothes."

She stood quite close to him, her eyes fixed on his face as if begging for his approval. She hurried on: "You look so much like Ben. Anybody would take you for him, if they hadn't known him as well as I did." She took a long breath. "Well, you know about me and Ben, but now he's gone, and you're the only part of him that's left. I never quit loving him, even when I didn't know how long he'd be in prison."

"I think he knew that," Ed said.

"I've been waiting for him. I thought he'd be here several days ago, but he didn't come, so I had to go back to Barger's ranch for some of my things. Gowdy thought you were Ben, so as soon as he saw you, he came after me."

He told her about the fight with the two men on his way here from Montrose. "From what they said, I figured they were Gowdy's men," he added.

"Barger's men," she corrected. "Clint Miller and Jake Simons, but Gowdy gave them their orders. He takes care of Barger's dirty work. That's what he was hired for three years ago. One of them was watching for Ben in Montrose, and the other one was camped down on Leopard Creek. I don't know what Gowdy told them to do, but I'm sure they weren't obeying orders when they jumped you. I'd guess they were going after the money themselves." She made a quick gesture, throwing out her hands to thrust all of this aside. "You haven't said whether you'd take me home with you. . . ."

"Not till after I find the money. I promised Ben I'd get it."

"Can you find it?"

"I told you I had a map."

"But you don't know the country. You'll be on Barger's range, and he's a bad man to have against you. If you do dodge him, you'll have to get horses, and you'll have to pack in grub and tools. The best thing to do is to get Barger on your side. He'd help you, if you're willing to let him have the ten thousand Ben promised to give him."

*Why not?* Ed thought. Forty thousand was enough, and Honey was going with him. She hadn't put it into words, but she might as well have said that if she couldn't have Ben, his brother would do.

"You want me to go to Barger's ranch in the morning?"

She nodded. "I'll help you hunt. I can save you time, because I know the country and I know the route Ben took after he left Gateway House." Impulsively she leaned forward and kissed him on the lips. "That's for Ed Morgan, not his brother, and it doesn't mean I'm grieving any the less for Ben. It's just that I want you to know I'm sorry for what I said and did a while ago."

He watched her walk to the gallery door. She opened it and turned her head to look at him. "Sleep as long as you want to in the morning. There's no hurry about starting to look for the money."

She went out, closing the door behind her. For a moment Ed stood motionless, knowing now why Ben had felt the way he had about her. She did turn a man inside out. "She'll do it to you," Ben had said. And she had. She was going back to the upper Laramie with him, and it hadn't been important to her whether he found the money or not. He went back to bed, knowing that as long as he lived, he would never forget the kiss she had given him.

# Chapter Five

Ed stirred briefly at dawn when the freighters harnessed up and drove out of the yard. He heard the clatter of hoofs on the plank floor of the bridge, the creak of heavily loaded wagons, the crunching of wheels, and the shouted curses of the drivers. He went back to sleep, and it was mid-morning before he woke again.

He dressed and rubbed his stubble-covered face, thinking of Honey Travers. He had never met a woman before who had hit him the way Honey had. Again he thought of what Ben had said—"She turns a man inside out, and she'd do it to you. . . ." And Grace Doane had said: "She's got a way of making you crazy." They were right. He'd been with Honey only a few minutes, but it had been long enough. Now the fever was in him.

He walked to the gallery door, opened it, and stepped out, wondering if Honey was in her room. He could go to her door and find out, but it wouldn't do, possessed as he was by the hunger that gripped him. Besides, she was probably downstairs, having breakfast.

For a time he stood there, feeling the cool mountain breeze that flowed up the cañon. Now, with the morning sunlight upon it, the yard below him looked like any of a dozen trailside places he had seen: the hock-deep dust, the sprawling log barn, the slab sheds scattered haphazardly around it. The alfalfa in the narrow field along the river would have to be cut soon. Billy Lowe was doing something at the east end of the field, plugging a leak in the ditch, Ed judged. Then, as Ed watched, the old man leaned the shovel against the fence and walked toward the barn.

The aspens through which Grace had led Ed the night be-

56

fore crowded against the house. Above him the cliff was spotted with other clumps of the quakies, tiny leaves turning restlessly in the wind, and his eyes, raking the wall, were momentarily fixed on the red sandstone upthrust that made a barren streak halfway to the top.

He turned to look at the river, gray with tailings from the mills upstream; he stared at the bridge he had crossed last night. Lifting his head, he let his gaze follow the road that cut down over the divide between the San Miguel and the Diablo. That was the way he had come, the way Ben and Honey had come when they had first stopped at Gateway House.

Another road turned directly upstream at the north end of the bridge. It led, Ed supposed, to Sentinel and the mines on the headwaters of the Diablo. This must be the road Ben had followed on his wild ride after the hold-up, saddlebags heavy with the Casino's money. He would have been caught sooner than he had if Grace Doane had not let him have a fresh horse.

Ed pondered this a moment, thinking how nearly Ben had succeeded in getting away, and how everything—Honey's life as well as his—would have been changed if he had succeeded in reaching the state line. A question occurred to Ed then. Why hadn't Ben gone on downriver as he had apparently planned? Instead, he had swung south over Jansen Mesa, a roundabout route to Utah.

Perhaps it wasn't important. Or, if it was, Honey likely knew the answer. He put the question out of his mind, thinking how aptly Grace's father had named his place Gateway House. He must have made a fortune here. He had died not long ago, according to what Hamp had said last night, and now, thinking about it, Ed could not understand why Grace wanted to get out, why Dal Barger would have anything to do with her running this place.

He turned and went back into his room, stirred by a sudden burst of impatience. No use lingering. Honey had made his course clear, and she had cut away the cause for fear that Grace Doane had planted in his mind. He opened his war sack and took razor, brush, and a cake of soap from it, thinking he would be seeing Honey in a few minutes. He remembered how Ruth had made him shave at least twice a week.

"I didn't marry a brush pile," she had often said. "I'll stay on my side of the bed, if you don't think enough of me to shave."

As he carried his shaving gear to the bureau, he saw the folded piece of paper that had been shoved under the door. Probably from Grace, he thought wryly, maybe a bill for a meal and the room, if Honey hadn't paid. But when he opened it, he saw that it was from Honey. He read:

**Dear brother of Ben,**

**I couldn't sleep after I left you because everything changed for me when you told me he was gone. I have lived for the moment when he would come to me again. This last week has been the longest week of my life, watching for him every day as I have, but now you've told me he'll never come back. I'm leaving Gateway House forever, and I'll never see it again. I will always remember that this is where it started, all the things that led to his imprisonment and death. It's a nightmare that I must forget when I leave with you. I'll tell Barger you're coming, and he'll furnish us with horses and the other things we'll need. Fishhook is about three hours from Gateway House. Take the road south of the river and you'll have no trouble finding the ranch.**

**Affectionately yours,**
**Honey Travers**

**P.S. I know what Grace Doane will say to you before you leave. Please trust me, Ed. If you do, you will not believe anything she tells you about me. I don't know why she hates me the way she does, but perhaps she was in love with Ben, too.**

**Honey**

He slipped the note into his shirt pocket, feeling let down because he had expected to see Honey this morning. He shaved, trying to ignore this feeling that could not be ignored. No other woman, not even Ruth, had affected him the way Honey Travers did.

He put his shaving gear away, trying to understand what it was about Honey that did this to him, but there was no explanation. A few days before he would have said it couldn't happen, for he had been convinced there would never be another woman after Ruth. Buying a woman for a single night was one thing, a dollars-and-cents bargain that would be finished and behind him. He didn't want Honey that way. He wanted her the rest of his life, to take care of her, to dream and plan with her as he had with Ruth. Ben had wanted it that way. Ed had no doubt of that.

He picked up his war sack and put his hat on, then he stopped, struck by a new thought that sent a crazy, sick feeling crawling through his belly. If Honey affected him that way, she would do the same to other men. Dal Barger would want her, too. According to Grace Doane, there was a question about which Barger wanted the most, Honey or the fifty thousand.

Ed left the room and went down the stairs, plagued again by the familiar uneasiness that he had felt so many times since he had left Montrose. After he met Barger, he would have some idea how to deal with the man, but now he was afraid of

59

the unknown. He didn't know what to expect.

For a moment he was tempted to forget the whole business; he'd saddle his buckskin and get to hell out of the country. Fifty thousand dollars wasn't worth getting killed over. But he knew at once he wouldn't do anything of the kind. Not with Honey counting on him.

When he reached the lobby, he saw that Billy Lowe had come in and was sweeping out the room. Lowe stopped to lean on the broom handle, his craggy face breaking into a mocking grin.

"All cleaned up, ain't you, Morgan?" Lowe said. "Cleaned up nice and pretty. Last night I couldn't see your mug on account of your whiskers."

"It was dark," Ed said, dropping his war sack behind the desk and laying his hat on it. "How about some breakfast?"

Lowe jabbed a finger toward the dining room. "Go sit down and see what happens. If it was me, I'd throw you out, but Grace ain't built that way. She'll fix you up with a bait of grub, though I tell her she's too good to stray pups and bastards like you that come drifting through here."

If Billy Lowe had been twenty years younger, Ed would have knocked him flat on his back. He glared at the old man, fighting his sudden burst of temper. There was something contemptuous in Lowe's faded eyes, in the sour grin that curled at the bottom of his brown-lipped mouth. Ed turned on his heel and walked into the dining room, his anger dying. Maybe the old man was tired. Or had indigestion.

The dining room had one long table, its oilcloth top scrubbed until it glistened. Ed pulled back a chair and sat down as a white-haired woman came out of the kitchen. For a moment she stared at him with cool disregard for his feelings. Then she said, as if a little surprised at her discovery: "You look a lot like Ben Morgan. You do for a fact."

"I'm hungry," Ed said impatiently.

"Hold your horses, mister. If you're so all-fired hungry, why didn't you get up and eat with the men?"

The woman might be Billy Lowe's wife. Or Hamp's. She was about their age and as careless of her manners as Lowe had been. Curiosity stirred in Ed as he wondered about the set-up in Gateway House. It took a great deal of labor to run a place like this, and he wondered why Grace Doane hired people who were too old to do a day's work.

Still the woman stood there, coldly appraising him, and again he felt the tug of anger. He rose. "I ain't so hungry I've got to be kicked in the teeth."

"Sit down," the woman said. "Sit down and tuck your shirt tail inside your pants and keep it there where it belongs. I'll fix you some bacon and eggs. Or maybe you want steak?"

"Sure, I'll have steak."

The woman laughed. "You'll have bacon and eggs, friend. I'll put the bacon on and go call Grace. She wants to talk to you, although I'm blessed if I know why."

She pushed through the swinging door into the kitchen. Ed dropped back into the chair, an explanation by Billy Lowe's change in attitude coming to him. Last night Lowe had thought he was Ben, but Grace must have told her people he wasn't. Ben had been respected, but a stranger pretending he was Ben would not merit respect. Well, it didn't make any difference. He'd be done with Gateway House within the hour.

Grace came into the dining room from the kitchen. She said—"Good morning."—in a cool, reserved tone.

Ed said—"Howdy."—and waited until she came to the opposite side of the table and sat down. Then he asked: "Why don't you fire the worn-out old has-beens you've got working for you?"

"It's none of your business," she said, "but I'll tell you. In the first place, I want folks I can trust. These folks who work for me used to work for Dad. I've known them as long as I can remember."

"Is there a second place?"

She nodded, tapping the table irritably. "A very good second place. Barger skims off the cream of what I make. I can't afford anyone else."

Her small, pointed chin was thrust defiantly at him as if she expected him to argue. She was wearing a blue dress that went well with her coloring, and there was a string of crystal beads around her tan throat. Her face, too, showed that she spent most of her daylight hours in the sunshine.

It occurred to Ed that Grace was the kind who liked to work outdoors, leaving the cooking and serving and cleaning to her help. She would be more attractive, he thought, if she took time with her hair, but it was pulled tightly back from her forehead and pinned in a bun on her neck in the way of a woman who is indifferent to her appearance.

He lowered his gaze under her hard scrutiny and reached for tobacco and papers. He said: "I'm Ed Morgan, Ben's brother."

"I'm not knocked out of my chair with surprise," she said. "Where's Ben?"

"He's dead."

That did surprise her. She said—"I'm sorry."—and paused as if uncertain what to say. Then she asked: "How did it happen?"

He told her, adding: "He didn't mention you or any deal he'd made with you, but he told me about Honey, and he wanted her to have her share."

The woman brought his breakfast: coffee, biscuits, a pitcher of syrup, and a thick plate loaded with fried eggs and bacon. She said: "Meals at odd times cost twice the usual price, mister."

"Go on back into the kitchen, Lissa," Grace said sharply. "He doesn't owe us anything."

Lissa whirled and stalked back through the swing door. Ed asked: "Why don't I owe you anything?"

"Honey paid for it already. She said you'd be leaving for Fishhook. I presume you had an exciting night."

"It's like you to say that."

"All right, you think I've got a dirty mind!" she exclaimed. "Well, maybe I have, and I know a dirty woman when I see one, but I'm not going to waste my breath trying to convince you what Honey is. Right now you think she's an angel. You do, don't you?"

"She doesn't have any wings, and neither do you," Ed said testily. "Ben told me he loved her, and he asked me to find the money so I could give some of it to her. That's what I aim to do."

"You think I'm lying when I say I have a half interest in anything you find?"

He began to eat, his eyes on the plate. "I told you Ben didn't mention you."

"He would have, if he'd had time," she said. "He probably knew he was dying, so he just told you what was uppermost in his mind. That would be Honey." She was silent for a time, watching him eat, then she said: "Ben was here for quite a while before he went to Sentinel, and he talked to me a lot. He said I was easier to talk to than Honey. Nothing interested her but love and money. That gets tiresome after a while."

"I reckon," he said.

"He was jealous of Barger even then, before he had any reason to be," she went on, "but he was awfully young, and he'd never been in love before. He didn't know how to hold

63

Honey, and it worried him. Anyhow, after he robbed the Casino, he came here, and I gave him a meal and my black gelding. He was on the run then, but he was crazy mad at Barger, mad enough to kill him."

"Why didn't he keep going down the river? Wasn't that the shortest way to Utah?"

"Didn't he tell you?"

"No.

"Two of Barger's men tried to stop him and take the money, but he killed them. He knew what Barger was up to then, so he was all for going to Fishhook and shooting Barger. I talked him out of it. He was bound to have a posse on his tail, and the best thing to do was to get away. I told him to come back after everything cooled down."

He gave her a quick glance, uncertain how much of this was the truth. If she weren't lying, he had a debt to settle with Barger, but it could wait until he'd found the money. Besides, he wanted to ask Honey about it.

He finished his meal and, leaning back in his chair, rolled himself a smoke. "Honey tells me I won't have any trouble with Barger. I wish I knew what kind of an *hombre* he really is."

"I told you last night," she said sharply. "And I'll tell you something else. You will have trouble with him, more trouble than you ever saw, but there's no use trying to talk you out of going. You could find that money with my help and get away, but, no, you've got to stick your neck into a loop and hand the rope over to Barger so he can throw it over a limb and pull. You're hooked, Morgan, hooked good."

He studied her through the drifting smoke of his cigarette. He asked: "Why are you under Barger's thumb?"

"Dad borrowed money from him, so he's got a mortgage on Gateway House. The interest is damned high. If I

64

miss a payment, he takes over."

"I don't savvy that. Why should Barger want Gateway House, if he's got a big spread?"

"He wants anything that pays. Gateway House would be a gold mine to him because he'd fetch in all the gambling gadgets you ever heard of." She leaned forward, fingertips drumming on the table top. "I'll tell you exactly what Barger is. He's a dead-ringer for Honey. He'll have a smile all over his face while he's fixing to stick a knife into your back. Honey has two gods. Barger has just one . . . money. A lot of it."

"What does he want it for?"

She rose, kicking her chair away with a vicious back swing of her foot. "I said it wrong. His god is himself. Money will buy the things he wants. He's no good, Morgan, just plain no good, but he's like a snake that hypnotizes you. That's why I've got to get out of here."

There was more to this than she was telling him, he thought, far more than the mere fact Barger held a mortgage on Gateway House, but he saw that she was in no mood to talk about it. Besides, it didn't concern him.

"I'll be riding," he said, and got up.

"I wish I could make you believe me," she said. "For your sake I wish I could."

"For my sake," he said harshly. "Why don't you quit trying to fool me? All you want is to wangle a deal for half the money. This way you know you can't."

"All right, I'll admit that, but it isn't the whole truth. I wouldn't give a damn about you if you weren't Ben's brother. You're a dead pigeon the minute you walk into Barger's house."

He remembered Honey saying in her letter that Grace might have been in love with Ben. Now he half believed it. He asked: "You'd go off and leave Gateway House if you had twenty-five thousand?"

"That's what I'd do," she cried passionately. "I'd do it just to get away from Barger."

He turned and left the dining room, thinking there was no use to keep talking to her. He saw that Billy Lowe was gone. He put on his hat and picked up his war sack, unaware that Grace had followed him until he swung toward the front door.

She said: "Morgan, I'm a prophet. Do you want to hear me prophesy?"

"No."

She moved in front of him and stood facing him, angry and defiant. "You'll listen anyhow. You'll tell them where the money is and they'll kill you. Or maybe they'll let you find the money, and then they'll kill you. Either way, you'll wind up in hell because you're so damned stubborn you won't listen to me." He started toward the door. She grabbed him by the arm, shouting at him. "Maybe you'll be lucky and get away after you get your eyes open! If you do, come back here. I'll still help you."

"For half?"

"That's fair, isn't it?"

"And maybe it would be fair if you shot me in the back so you'd get all of it."

"Go to hell!" she screamed, releasing her grip on his arm. "I'll dance on your coffin, if they'll let me come to your funeral."

"I'll ask Barger to invite you," he said, and left the house.

# Chapter Six

Hamp was not in the barn when Ed reached it. He saddled his buckskin, lashed the war sack into place behind the cantle, then mounted, reined his horse around the barn, and started up the shelf road that led to Jansen Mesa. Red dust stirred by the buckskin's hoofs drifted slowly away from the wall of the cañon. The sun, noon high, filled the mountain air with a dry, brittle heat.

In spite of himself, Ed could not free his mind of the doubt that Grace Doane had planted there. What she had said about Ben's reason for turning south from the river made sense. If it was true, everything else she said that night might be equally true.

A malicious fate had tangled his twine for him, even to keeping him from reaching Montrose on time. Ben had mailed the letter with days to spare, but a storm had washed the road out, and the stage had been delayed.

If he had reached Montrose on time, Ben would have had days of life instead of hours; he would have had time to tell about Barger and Grace. Now Ed had to make a choice. If he trusted Honey, he could not believe Grace. Conversely, if he believed Grace, he could not trust Honey. But as he thought about it, he realized that he had no problem. He wanted to trust Honey.

He drew Ben's map from his pocket and studied it, carefully fixing in his mind the relation of the falls to the spot where the money was hidden. The two pines, the red-rimrock with its streaks of yellow. He struck a match and held it to the paper; he watched it flame and curl and grow black, holding to one corner as long as he could; then he blew out the last small flame and wiped the charcoal remnants against his pants leg. This was his life insurance. He should have burned the map before he left Montrose.

From now on he must rely entirely upon his memory. Probably there were a thousand pines along the south rim of Jansen Mesa, probably miles of red rock with yellow streaks. Finding a needle in a haystack might be easy compared to the task that faced him.

Suddenly it occurred to him that Grace had succeeded in making him more suspicious of Honey than he had realized, or he wouldn't have burned the map. He swore softly, remembering Honey's letter: **Please trust me, Ed. If you do, you will not believe anything she tells you about me.** Still the doubt lingered in his mind.

Within the hour he reached the top. The Cañon of the Diablo was a great twisting trench to his right, the cottonwoods in the bottom toy-size, the river a silver ribbon. The road swung sharply away from the rim to cut through a thick forest of piñons. A quarter of a mile farther on he came into the open. Jansen Mesa lay before him, covered by grass and sagebrush with here and there a lonely, wind-bent cedar, endless miles of range that would please the heart of any cattleman.

Pulling up, Ed hipped around in the saddle. To the east the crest of the San Juan Mountains lay against the horizon, a series of jagged peaks that bit into the stainless sky like the teeth of a giant saw. No mountains were visible to the south, just rimrock marking the edge of the mesa, a seemingly endless line that was made hazy by distance and shifting heat waves.

Somewhere below that rim were the two pine trees with fifty thousand dollars in gold and greenbacks hidden between them. If there was the slightest truth in what Grace Doane had said, Dal Barger was anything but an honest man. And

Honey? Here it was again. He rolled a cigarette, lighted it, and broke the match between thumb and forefinger, trying to think of her with the calm detachment he should have for a woman he had met but a few hours before.

It was impossible. No man who had been kissed by her could regard her with cool detachment. Ben had called her a bitch, and in the same breath he'd said he loved her. Whatever she had done to Ben had not killed his love. But perhaps she had not actually done anything to Ben. Maybe Grace Doane had written to him and had stirred doubt in him just as she had in Ed. How was a man to know?

Swearing softly, Ed wheeled his horse off the road and took a westward course through the sagebrush. He'd locate the falls before he went on to Fishhook. He'd find the money, give Barger his share, and leave the country with Honey. It was that simple.

La Sals Range lay ahead of him across miles of broken country, a solid clump of mountains still holding a frosting of snow. Somewhere over there was the Utah line. Ben had not been far from it when the posse had caught him. The thought occurred to Ed that Ben had had no control over his own destiny. It had been shaped by the choices he had made in the past. Suddenly Ed was haunted by the weird feeling that he could not shape his own life, that fate in the form of fifty thousand dollars had taken it out of his hands.

A mile from the road Ed turned to the rim and forced his buckskin through the piñon forest. The cañon was deeper here than where he had climbed out of it, and the falls were not yet in sight. He rode back through the piñons and turned westward again, wondering about the absence of human life. Jansen Mesa was too big for one ranch, and the grass was better here than where he'd first come out of the cañon. The fact that there were no other ranches bore out what Grace had said about Dal Barger. This was isolated country, tucked far down into the southwestern corner of Colorado's western slope, but isolation never kept cattlemen from moving onto a new range. Force would do it, if the force was great enough, and, judging from the echoing solitude, Barger's force had been sufficient.

A second mile dropped behind, then a third, and again Ed pushed through the fringe of piñons to the rim. Not far west of this point the river disappeared into what seemed a bottomless hole. Even at this distance Ed could hear the muted rumble of the plunging stream. Here were the falls Ben had mentioned.

He followed the cañon for fifty yards or more, and pulled up. Below him the slick-rock rim dropped off a sheer hundred feet, then the brush-covered walls tapered more gradually to the bottom. Now Ed understood why Ben had said he'd have to locate the falls from the rim. At this point neither horse nor man could have climbed from the river to the top.

He swung southward, finding that the piñon forest had widened. He rode into an arroyo and came out of it, circling a hodgepodge of slab rock, and unexpectedly found himself in a clearing that held a small ranch. A man stepped out of the stone cabin, a Winchester held on the ready.

Ed reined up, one look at the cowman's bruised face telling him that this might be trouble. He said—"Howdy."—and waited. The man moved toward him, dust rising from his worn boots, then he stopped, his gaze locked with Ed's. Now, with not more than ten feet between them, Ed saw that the man's right eye was swelled shut, his nose had been smashed into a bloody pulp, and his lips were puffy. Ed had stumbled into something that was no concern of his. He said: "I'm heading for Fishhook. How do I go from here?"

"South," the man said thickly. "Straight south to

Fishhook and hell, as if you didn't know."

"I don't. This is new country to me."

The man snorted derisively. "You look to me like another one of Barger's gun-slinging bastards."

"Not me. I'm just riding through."

"Then keep riding, or I'll blow your guts out through your backbone."

"I like my guts where they are," Ed said, and would have ridden on if the man hadn't said: "Wait."

"I didn't come here for trouble," Ed said. "I told you I was just riding through."

"Nobody tells the truth on this range. You might be lying. Maybe Barger sent you here to see if I'd pulled my freight."

"I never saw Barger in my life. I don't know nothing about your politics."

"Politics, hell," the rancher shouted. "This ain't politics. It's murder. Savvy? Murder, so I'm pulling out because I'm scared. I never bothered Barger. I was just a Johnny-come-lately with a few cows and half a dozen horses, but Barger says I've got to git. All right, I'll git, and leave him my cows and horses, damn his soul to hell."

The man was young, probably no older than Ed. He had been beaten, and now he was panicky and dangerous. Ed said nothing. Anything might stir the fellow into a killing rage, and all Ed wanted was to get out of here. He glanced past the man at the pole corrals, the low shed, and a small pile of fire-wood beside the front of the house. Everything about the place indicated poverty, the poverty of a man who possessed nothing but his hands, a few head of stock, and hope. Now he had only his hands.

"I'm Rufe Nason," the man said. "Can you remember that?" When Ed nodded, he went on: "You say you're a stranger heading for Fishhook. Maybe you're lying, maybe

71

not. Don't make no big difference. I just want you to tell Barger something."

"Sure, I'll tell him."

"A promise don't mean nothing on this range, neither, but if you are a stranger, you ain't scared yet, so maybe you'll tell him." Nason's shirt front stirred with the depth of his breathing, his one good eye pinned on Ed's face. "Tell him he ain't God because God would be man enough to hold his woman. Tell him I've seen her on the trail with Spur Gowdy more'n once."

Ed went cold inside. But this Nason might not mean Honey. He asked hoarsely: "What woman?"

"Hell, there's only one woman on Fishhook. Barger thinks he owns her, but he don't. That's the only way he can be hurt, and by God I want him hurt. Tell him he can have his toughs beat hell out of me, but he can't hold his woman. Will you tell him that?"

The rifle barrel lifted another six inches so that it was lined on Ed's chest. Nason was breathing hard, his bruised face dark with his hatred. Time played out. Nason's finger tightened on the trigger, but at that moment Ed could not find his voice.

"It's a fair trade," Nason said bitterly. "Your life, if you tell him that. I'm getting out tonight. Tell him that, too, if you want to."

The man was crazy, his pride and his ambition beaten out of him. Only a wild desire to strike back at Barger's weak spot remained. "I'll tell him," Ed said.

"Then start riding. Straight south. Stay here long enough and you'll be afeared to go."

"I'm going," Ed said, and rode past the man and on across the clearing.

A moment later he was in the piñons again. He did not

look back, not until he was past the trees, and, when he did, he could not see the stone house. Then he began to tremble. He thought about Grace's saying that anybody who lived in Jansen Mesa or the Diablo was under Dal Barger's shadow.

He went on, the sun in the west now, and gradually his panic passed. He had wanted to know what sort of man Barger was. Now he knew. Only one kind of man would do what Barger had done to Rufe Nason. But what Nason had said about Honey might not be true. Probably he had made it up in the hope he could exact some small revenge for what Barger had done to him. Or it might not mean anything, if it were true. There was no harm in Honey's meeting Spur Gowdy on the trail.

Harm! Hell, what difference did it make? Ed was no guardian of Honey's morals. It was her business if she was Barger's woman. She was willing to take part of the money, but that was understandable. Ben had wanted her to have it.

Still, the queasy uneasiness remained in Ed's belly, and he knew the reason for it. Barger, as Grace had said, might not be satisfied with ten thousand. A man of his caliber would want it all. Too, Ed had been counting on Honey's leaving the mesa with him, but Barger would stop her, if he could.

Ed rode due south, the sun dipping lower in the west. He considered getting off the mesa while he could, going back to Grace and taking whatever help she could give him. Or he might circle the ranch and have a try at it himself. But he had nothing to dig with, and he didn't have any grub. If Barger found him, there was no doubt what the man would do. It was better, he decided, to deal with Barger when the time came. There would be no danger until the money was found.

Glancing back, Ed located a notch in the divide between the Diablo and the San Miguel. Directly ahead of him there was a sandstone spire that pointed skyward like a great finger.

From here it appeared that the spire rose from the south rim. The money should be on this side of it, probably not far away, and on a line between the notch and the spire.

The ranch came into view suddenly in the bottom of a valley that ran east and west, its course marked by a heavy growth of willows that crowded its banks. As he rode down the slant, Ed saw that Barger had built well, with an eye to the future. The house was made of stone, a two-story rectangular structure. The bunkhouse, corrals, sheds, and a sprawling stone barn lay west of the house.

Ed reached the creek, hearing its murmur behind the willows, and reined toward the house. A couple of horses were racked in front, more were in the near corral, and, now that he was close, Ed had the impression that this was a well-run outfit, neat and clean and efficient.

Most ranches, including his own, always had some loose odds and ends around so that they gave the appearance of needing a long-overdue clean-up. But no loose odds and ends were visible here. There was not a tree in sight, no pretense of a lawn, no flowers. A working ranch without the slightest trace of a woman's presence, and Ed found himself wondering how Honey had liked the four years she'd spent here.

She'd had to make a living, she'd said, but it might have been a prison for her while she'd waited for Ben to come back. Then he realized with a sudden rush of bitterness that he had no way of knowing how she really felt, that he was simply hoping she wanted to get away. If she had been seeing Spur Gowdy. . . . Hell, it was her business. He had to keep telling himself that.

Ed reined up at the horse trough and dismounted as a man came out of the barn. Ed let his buckskin drink as he watched the man approach. He was big, with saber-sharp nose and a sweeping black mustache that must have taken half a lifetime to grow and was probably the source of his greatest pride.

"You Morgan?" the man asked in a friendly tone.

"Yeah, I'm Morgan."

The buckskin lifted his head and snorted. The man gave the animal a long, speculative stare. He said approvingly: "Good animal."

"I raised him," Ed said. "I've got a little spread on the upper Laramie."

Ed wasn't sure the man heard. He nodded absently, and said again: "Good animal." He glanced at Ed. "Is he for sale?"

"Not for a million dollars."

The man grinned. "Well, now, maybe for a hundred dollars cash?"

"No."

"Don't blame you. Go on in. I'll take care of your horse. Miss Travers said you'd be along, so the boss is expecting you." The man held out his hand. "I'm Lou Riddle. If you're around for a spell, we'll get acquainted. I do the chores hereabouts, some of 'em easy and some more that are down right hard and dirty."

Ed shook hands with him. "Glad to know you," he said, and wondered what Riddle had meant when he'd said chores. He looked more like a fighter than a man who had been hired to clean the stables.

Riddle's red-flecked eyes swung down Ed's lanky body and lifted to his face. He said: "Tough country, Mister Morgan, real tough. Not much like your Laramie Valley. I was there once. Right purty, as I remember it. Well, go on in."

Ed watched Riddle lead the buckskin toward the corral, asking himself why Riddle had told him it was a tough country. He swung to the trough and sloshed water over his sweat-crusted face. He was getting boogery, he decided. Probably Riddle hadn't meant anything. Isolated as it was, Fishhook would have few visitors. Chances were the man was lonesome and had been merely making talk.

Ed wiped his sleeve across his face and rubbed his hands on his pants. Suddenly he had the feeling he was being watched. He glanced at the bunkhouse but saw no one; he turned his eyes to the stone house and caught the flutter of a curtain at an upstairs window. He grinned as he started toward the house. Honey, he thought. He had taken longer to get here than she had expected.

As he stepped up on the porch, the front door swung open. A man said in a warm, cordial voice: "Welcome to Fishhook, Mister Morgan. Come in."

He was looking at Dal Barger.

# Chapter Seven

Barger was the kind of man who, once seen, could not be easily forgotten, but at the moment Ed was not sure what there was about the fellow that made such an impact upon him. Barger was not big, yet somehow he contrived to give an impression of bigness. He was not handsome in the way a man's appearance was ordinarily measured; his features were too perfect, so perfect that they might have belonged to a woman. Still, there was nothing effeminate about him.

He was the personification of confident strength. That was it, Ed thought. Somehow Dal Barger, without making a threatening gesture or saying a word, was able to convey the feeling that no human being was strong enough to prevent him from attaining anything he wanted.

Ed moved across the porch and shook Barger's hand. The palm was soft, but the grip was firm, Barger's eyes meeting Ed's. "I'm late," Ed said. "Overslept this morning."

Smiling, Barger said: "I understand, Mister Morgan. Sit down. I'll get you a drink."

For just a moment Barger stood motionless, dark eyes searching Ed's face as if probing his mind. Then, apparently satisfied, he swung toward a sideboard, picked up a bottle of whisky, and filled two glasses. Staring at the man's austere, arrow-straight back, Ed had the weird feeling that Barger had successfully picked his mind of every thought that was there.

The impression of vast power that Barger gave Ed grew as the man came back across the room. He was immaculately clad in a black broadcloth suit, white silk shirt, and string tie. His expensive boots were black and polished to a high glow, a black-butted Colt was visible under the skirt of his coat. Every motion he made was smooth and rhythmic; he possessed the cat-like grace of a man who was deadly fast with his gun.

Barger handed Ed's glass to him and, lifting his own, bowed slightly and smiled. "Here's to a successful search for wealth, Mister Morgan."

They drank, and Ed gave the glass to Barger who returned it to the sideboard. Glancing around, the thought struck Ed that this was the strangest living room he had ever seen. Heavy beams crossed the ceiling; the walls were oak paneling. The original cost of the dark, massive furniture must have added up to a small fortune.

The overall impression that the room had been designed to give a visitor was one of studied elegance. Ed felt awkward and out of place, although there was nothing in Barger's courteous manner that should have given him that feeling. Still, it was there, and, as he reached for tobacco and papers and rolled a smoke, he thought that what he knew about Barger did not seem to fit the actual appearance of the man. But the devil, of course, was not likely to resemble the devil.

"Sit down," Barger said. "Honey will be along in a few minutes."

"I've been sitting most of the day," Ed said. "It feels good to stand."

He moved to the cavernous fireplace that made up most of the east wall of the room and tossed his charred match into it. Barger had dropped down upon a black leather couch and was lighting a cigar. The momentary silence that lay between them was a cool, impenetrable wall. Ed, standing with his back to the fireplace, felt his uneasiness grow until it lay like a cold blade against his spine.

"I'm sorry about Ben's death," Barger said. "I knew him pretty well, and I liked him. Or let's say I liked his guts. I play a great deal of poker, usually for high stakes, and I pride myself on being a good player, but Ben trimmed me. You might be interested to know that it was the only bad beating I ever took at cards in my life."

"But it brought him bad luck," Ed said.

Barger nodded agreement. "You can't blame me for that. I did save his life, you know. This fellow, Vance, who owned the Casino was a killer. Ben spotted his crooked dealing, when I was playing Vance, and he made the mistake of calling him."

"Why was it a mistake?"

"The town of Sentinel belonged to Vance. It's a mining camp, and everything centered around the Casino. You know, good liquor, the best girls, the big games. The mine owners never went anywhere else, and most of the buying and selling of claims took place there. Naturally Vance couldn't allow Ben to make his accusation stick. His men jumped Ben and threw him into the alley. If I hadn't taken him to my hotel room, he'd have been killed."

Ed finished his cigarette and threw the stub into the fireplace. Barger toyed with his cigar, his eyes on it. He went on: "I called Honey into my room, and, when Ben came around, we talked it over. He didn't have a nickel left, so he was all for smoking it out with Vance. It would have been suicide, so I got him to wait until the next night when I could arrange for a relay of horses down the river. I told him the only way he'd get his money back was to take it with a gun. He did, and he got away. It was just bad luck that his horse threw a shoe."

Ed remained silent, wondering why Barger was telling him this. Then he remembered what Grace had said about Barger's men trying to take Ben's money from him, but there was no use bringing it up now. True or not, Barger would deny it.

"I did what I could for Ben at the trial," Barger went on,

"and I succeeded in getting a light sentence for him." He pulled on his cigar, frowning thoughtfully. "I said I had a lot of respect for Ben's guts. He showed it at the trial. He'd have got off easy if he'd told Vance where the money was, but he wouldn't talk. I call that guts, Morgan, damned tough guts."

"What happened to Vance?"

"He was shot in a saloon brawl a few months after the trial. He had no heirs, so nobody has a better right to the money than you have"—Barger paused, and then added—"unless it's Honey. Ben was very fond of her. It has been a pleasure to me to provide a home for her. She and Ben planned to get married and join you, so it seems to me that it's only fair for her to receive part of the money."

"She'll get it, if I find it. Might be hard to find, though. I don't know this country."

"Honey said you had a map."

"Wasn't much of a map. Ben said the money was south of the falls. I located them today." Ed pinned his eyes on Barger's face. "Ran into a fellow named Rufe Nason. Looked like he'd got a bad beating."

"He was hard to persuade." Barger rose and, coming to the fireplace, stood with a hand on the mantel. "Men like Nason are petty nuisances. As a cattleman, you know how it is. Fishhook is the biggest spread in this part of Colorado. I came here years ago, not long after the Utes were driven out. Just a kid with a few cows and a lot of ambition. Well, I'm thirty-five now, and I have a right to be proud of what I've done. I refuse to share my range with a pack of ten-cow ranchers who live on my beef while they ship their own."

"He was crazier'n a hoot owl," Ed said. "Had a Winchester on me all the time I was there. Figured you'd sent me to find out if he'd left. He said he was pulling out tonight."

"Good. I was afraid I might have trouble with him." Steps

sounded on the stairway at the far end of the room. Barger turned, smiling. "Come on down, Honey."

She paused on the third step, her head held high and proud. Her smile was for Ed as she stood there, ignoring Barger, fully conscious of her beauty and seeking Ed's approval. She was wearing a red satin dress, the bodice cut so that it made a close fit over the high swell of her breasts; the skirt flared out tantalizingly at the knee-line in a manner that would instinctively bring a man's eyes to her.

Now, looking at Honey in the late afternoon sunlight from a west window, Ed had the impression that this was her finest dress that would be worn only on special occasions. From the manner in which her blue-green eyes caressed him, he felt that it was his presence that made it a special occasion. Pride touched him with a warm glow. Honey Travers possessed both dignity and beauty, a fact he had not been fully aware of the night before.

"I'm glad you're here, Ed," Honey said, and came on down the stairs.

"You're very pretty."

At the moment it was all Ed could say. She said—"Thank you."—and walked to the couch, her skirt rustling with each step. She sat down, the smile lingering at the corners of her mouth. She turned her gaze to Barger. "You see, Dal, I have at least one admirer."

"You have more than one," he said quickly. "You know that."

She leaned back, her hands folded on her lap. Her yellow hair was pinned in a high crown on her head. Now she stirred restlessly as if holding within herself some feeling she did not want Barger to share, her eyes turning again to Ed. He lowered his gaze, flushing, conscious of his worn, range clothes.

Barger was amused, Ed thought, Barger in his fine clothes and big house that spoke so loudly of his wealth. Fifty thousand dollars, even if it were in Ed's pocket, would be a piddling amount set against Barger's fortune. Honey had everything she wanted right here. It was a bitter thought that left its sourness in his mind.

"I'm glad to hear my admirers are not limited to one," Honey said.

"She's laughing at me," Barger said to Ed. "I've asked her many times to marry me, but Ben was always between us. Now you're here, and it's astonishing how much you resemble him. It's . . . it's almost as if his ghost was present."

A Chinese cook came into the room, bowing and saying: "Is lcady."

Honey rose. "I expect you're hungry, Ed."

"Sure, I can eat," he said, and followed Honey into the dining room.

But he wasn't hungry. It was wrong, all wrong and too grand. The great oak table covered by a linen cloth. Candlelight winking on the silver. Fragile, blue-flowered plates. Tall, delicate goblets he was afraid to touch. Wine that must have been a century old. Supper here in the middle of Jansen Mesa in a baronial splendor as fantastic as the miracle of a cactus blossom in a drab desert, unexplainable and unexpected and wrong for a visitor like Ed Morgan.

The talk was casual and impersonal, of mines at the head of the Diablo, grass in the high country below the crest of the San Juans, a hunting trip that Barger had made the year before, the mystery of a ghost that haunted the south rim. Ed listened and was silent, some inner monitor warning him that there was a danger here that had not yet taken definite shape or form.

When dessert was finished, Barger leaned back and

lighted a cigar. He said: "I suppose you're anxious to start the search, Morgan."

Ed nodded. "I've got to get back home."

"What sort of an outfit do you have?"

"Piddling."

"But with room to expand?"

"Lots of room."

"Good." Barger took the cigar out of his mouth and studied the dull glow. "You'll have Ben's money to expand with. Now there is one thing. I feel I should have the ten thousand I lost to Ben. Not that I have any legal claim. I lost it fair enough, but I think I should have it in exchange for the help I'll be glad to give you."

"That's fair," Ed said.

"Well, then, that's fine," Barger said as if relieved. "I'll send a man with you in the morning who knows the country. You'll have a couple of pack animals with some grub, so you can stay out as long as you need to." He rose. "I have a little book work to do, so I'll leave you to entertain our guest, Honey."

Honey lifted her eyes to his face. "I'm going with him."

Irritated, Barger said: "You won't like it. They might be out a couple of weeks. Hard work and dust and camp grub with sand in it. That sound like fun?"

"I'm going."

Barger pulled on his cigar, frowning. "A stubborn woman is a trial to a man, Morgan. What's your feeling about it? I mean, having your work slowed down and delayed by female whims."

"I'll be glad to have her if she wants to go," Ed said.

Barger took the cigar from his mouth and fingered the gray ash into his coffee cup. "We haven't talked about Honey," he said. "I took her in when Ben went to prison. She had two choices . . . to make a living in Sentinel, and there was only one way she could do it . . . or to come here. I welcomed her because I like beauty, and she has been an ornament. As a matter of fact, that's all she has been."

Ed rose. "You want her to stay here? Is that what you're driving at?"

"Exactly," Barger answered. "Now what are your intentions regarding her? I mean, about the money?"

"I don't know. I mean, whatever she thinks is fair."

"And if she wants all of it?"

"You'll get your part."

"I see." Barger's eyes swung briefly to Honey's face and back to Ed's. "Well, we'll talk more about it after the money's found. Right now, I have work to do. I'll see that you're called at sunup."

Nodding, Barger left the room. Honey remained in her chair, her hands knotted on the table, her head bent forward so that Ed could not see her face. Barger's quick steps sounded across the living room and died; a door was slammed shut. Without saying an unfriendly word, he had succeeded in destroying the illusion of security he had previously built. Looking down at Honey, Ed wondered what was responsible for Barger's leaving in the manner he had.

"He'll stay in his office for hours," Honey said. "I often wonder what he does. He can't have that much book work to do."

Still she did not look at him. He stared down at the top of her head, her hair touched by the candlelight so that it seemed more golden than it was. Gold, he thought, the color of the money he had come here to find, and then he remembered that Ben had loved her, but had not fully trusted her. He said: "Honey."

She looked up. "I know what you're thinking," she said defiantly. "Go ahead and tell me you don't believe what Barger said about me being nothing more than an ornament to him."

He shook his head. "I was thinking about Ben. He said you were a bitch."

She stood up, strong feeling stirring her features. "He called me that to my face the last time I visited him in prison, but he shouldn't have believed what Grace Doane wrote. I don't think he did believe it, really, or he wouldn't have planned to come back to me." Her head tipped back in her proud way. "He couldn't live away from me, could he?"

"No," Ed answered. "I don't think he could."

"Can you?"

He turned from the table, not answering. He was thinking of Ruth, who had been so much different from Honey, Ruth, who had married him and died in a futile effort to give him a son. She had known she was dying as he sat beside the bed holding her hand, and, because she had known, she'd said: "You'll get married again. I want you to. You're the kind of man who needs a wife." But he hadn't seen another woman he'd wanted until he met Honey.

He walked to the window, refusing to give her the satisfaction of hearing his answer. It was dark now, the night pressing against the house. Honey came to stand beside him, laying a hand on his arm.

"I haven't told you how much I owe Ben," she said. "I was broke when I met him. I didn't have any place to go, and I couldn't find work. You know what would have happened to me if I hadn't gone with him. I told you last night I had known one good, decent man. I suppose it's too much to expect his brother to be as good."

He swung away from the window. "What are you trying to say?"

"I'm not very proud, Ed. Not with you. As long as Ben was alive, I had a future to look forward to, but now it's different. Unless I have you, I don't have anything."

"You know what you do to a man, don't you?"

"I guess so. I know women hate me, and men want me. Is that wrong, Ed?"

He couldn't answer. A man builds up an illusion about a woman, he thought. He wants to believe she's better than she is. He hadn't known anything about Ruth's past. He hadn't wanted to, so he had never asked her, but on the other hand he hadn't doubted her, at least not after they were married. But Honey? He was a man, and he wanted her. The right and the wrong of it made no difference. He looked at her, feeling the hunger for her grow until it was a flame in him.

He said—"I'd better get out to the bunkhouse."—and was not sure what he'd do if she told him that was where he'd sleep.

She shook her head, smiling a little. "Your room's upstairs. You're not sleepy yet, are you?"

"No."

"But you want to go to bed. So do I, in a minute." She jerked her head toward the living-room door. "Come on."

He followed her. The front door had been left open, and the air was clean and cool and richly spiced with sage smell. Honey lighted a lamp on the mahogany table and turned to him, not yet ready to go. She asked: "Do you like this room?"

"No."

"Neither do I, but it suits Barger. He likes size and expensive things. And darkness." She waved a hand around the room. "Furniture. His clothes. The butt of his gun. He even rides a black gelding. He brags about it. He says the devil likes

86

darkness, too." She walked to the sideboard, poured him a drink, and brought it to him. "I have never seen Barger bleed, but his blood must be as black as his soul." She moved to the front door and stood, looking out into the night, a shoulder against the jamb, her high breasts rising and falling with her breathing.

Ed sensed the bitter mood that possessed her. Presently he asked: "Why are you here?"

She was silent a long time, standing with her back to him. Then she said: "It's been a place to live, Ed. That's all. Just a place to wait for Ben. For four years I haven't had to worry about clothes or food or a place to sleep. I've had time to think about light, because there was so little here, and darkness because there was so much. And some of the time I wasn't sure which was which." She glanced over her shoulder at him. "Do you always know?"

He put his glass down and went to her. "Not any more."

"You used to, from what Ben said. He had a word for you. He said you were pious."

"All right, I've changed," he said roughly. "My wife changed me. Or maybe Ben did. Damn it, I wasn't made like him. I had to run the ranch, and it took work to do it. We'd have lost the outfit if I hadn't."

"But he didn't see it the way you did. Not until after I met him." He was standing quite close to her now, and she turned so that her shoulder touched him. "Funny about Ben. So much good and so much foolishness. He made the mistake of trusting the wrong man. If he'd lived long enough, he'd have killed Barger."

He waited, thinking of the issue that would be decided in the morning. He had taken Ben's place. He would kill Barger or be killed by him. Honey had been saying that in her indirect way, he thought, and she had been telling him, too, that

87

nothing would be left for her if he was the one who died. But why had she brought him here?

He put his hands on her arms, gripping them roughly. "A while ago we were going upstairs, but now we're not. Well, I'm going to do what Ben would, if he was here. I'm taking .you away from here. Now."

"We can't. Riddle's out there somewhere. Probably Lance, too. You haven't seen him, but he's like Riddle. Barger owns them. I don't know how or why, but he does."

"Gowdy?"

She bit her lower lip. "I suppose Grace Doane told you about him."

He nodded. "He was in the lobby when I signed the register."

"You couldn't tell much about him, just looking at him."

"I could tell quite a bit."

"But you listened to Grace, didn't you?" He nodded, and she went on. "Grace hates him. So does Barger, and he's afraid of Spur, if he's afraid of any man."

"Why does he keep him around?"

"Gowdy has the fastest gun on the western slope. Besides, he's good at handling men like Riddle and Lance. And the two you killed. The plain truth is, Barger needs him."

"Is Gowdy here?"

"He's probably in the bunkhouse." She stepped past him, then walked to the table, and picked up the lamp. She held it so the light was upon her face, her eyes mocking him. "You aren't really pious, are you, Ed? Not when it's you instead of Ben. And not when it comes to money or a woman."

In that moment he thought he hated her, and he understood why Ben had been in torment about her. What kind of woman was she? Then she was laughing, the dark mood gone from her.

"I thought so," she said.

She walked toward the stairs, confident that he would come, and the room was filled with the rustling of her satin dress.

# Chapter Eight

Ed followed Honey up the curving stairway and into a room on the east side of the hall. There was no hint of the luxury that dominated the living room downstairs. The furniture was simple and cheap: an iron bedstead, the paint peeling from it, a cane-bottom chair, and a pine bureau with a white bowl and pitcher.

She set the lamp on the bureau and stood looking at him, her full, rich lips slightly parted. He walked to her and reached for her with a rough, violent motion; he jerked her to him, and her arms came up around his neck, and her lips were sweet and hungry. Presently she pushed him away, trembling a little, and he realized she was thinking of Ben.

"It's no good, is it?" she asked. "Not yet, anyway."

He knew what she meant. She had been waiting for Ben, but Ben would never come for her. All that she could ever have of him was his brother, and he wouldn't do. She would use him to get her away from here. In time, he might take Ben's place in her heart, but it would be a long time, perhaps a very long time.

"I'll wait," he said.

She put a hand to her throat and walked around the room restlessly, glancing at him now and then. Finally she said: "Don't hate me, Ed. No matter what happens, don't hate me. Having you come here was my idea. I hope it was the right thing for you to do. I thought it was, but now I'm not sure."

She whirled and left the room. He ran after her and caught her by the arm just as she was opening her door across the hall. He said: "Hold on. Why are we waiting? The money isn't important. Let's get out of here in the morning."

She shook her head, smiling wryly. "Barger wouldn't let me go, Ed."

"Tonight, then."

She shook her head again, a little impatient now. "You don't understand. He would kill you before he'd let me go with you. Tonight. Tomorrow. Any time. The only thing we can do is to go after the money."

"That wouldn't change anything, if he's. . . ."

"Listen, Ed. He wants the money, and he wants me. He thinks he can have both. That's how we'll have our chance. We'll leave in the morning. He'll send Riddle or Lance with us. Maybe both. Barger won't make any trouble until after the money's found. If he keeps his word and is satisfied with the ten thousand, we'll be all right. If he isn't, you'll have to handle him when the time comes."

"I'll handle him," Ed said.

He'd handle Barger or kill him, he told himself. But he knew at once this was wishful thinking. Nothing more. He could not kill all of them. Barger, Spur Gowdy, Lance, Riddle. Perhaps the whole crew. He was in Barger's country. How could he get away with Honey when Barger wanted her?

"Good night, Ed," Honey said, and closed the door.

He waited a moment, but he did not hear the lock click. So she trusted him. He stood staring at the door, not at all sure she had any right to trust him. He rubbed a hand across his face. It came away damp with sweat. He turned slowly and went back into his own room and shut the door.

He sat down on the bed and rolled a cigarette. As he smoked, he thought about this, wishing again that Ben had had time to tell him more about Grace Doane and Barger. Now he was sure of only one thing. He was not leaving without Honey, no matter what Barger did or said.

He finished his cigarette and rolled another one. Long

odds, any way he looked at it. "Don't hate me," she had said. Well, he had trusted her, regardless of what Grace Doane had told him, but now Honey admitted she wasn't sure he had done the right thing, coming here and putting himself in Barger's hands as he had. Too late now to worry about having done the wrong thing. Maybe there was nothing to worry about, at least for a few days. They'd eat breakfast together in the morning, polite and friendly, and then start south, every one of them knowing that the instant the money was found there'd be hell to pay.

He took off his boots, shirt, and pants, and went to bed, but he could not sleep. Later—he had no idea how much later because time passed very slowly for him—he heard his door open. He sat up, reaching for his gun that was in the holster on the floor near the head of the bed.

"You awake, Ed?"

Honey! He lay back, taking a long breath of relief. "Yeah, I'm awake."

She came into his room and stood by the window. "I couldn't sleep," she said. "I've been thinking how so much money brings out the worst in people. If I had it to do over again, I'd have left Gateway House with you and forgotten about the money."

"I wouldn't have gone," he said. "I promised Ben."

"I know," she said bitterly. "I keep telling myself that's why I didn't ask you to leave. You're the kind who'd keep a promise if it killed you, aren't you?"

He didn't answer. She was right, but it seemed stupid to say it so bluntly. A promise to a dead man wasn't worth being killed over, but he was the way he was, stupid or not. He looked at her, the moonlight from the window falling upon her. She had put a robe on over her nightgown, and now, staring at the side of her face, he thought he had never seen a woman so beautiful as Honey Travers, or as desirable.

"Well, no use keeping you awake," she said. "No matter what happens in the morning, you've got to keep on the good side of Barger, if you can. If we have trouble, we don't want it here."

She left, closing the door behind her. She wasn't sure of Barger, he thought, and she was regretting her decision to bring him here. She must know more than she had told him, and he was tempted to get up and dress and have it out with her. If he had walked into a trap and had to fight his way out, he'd better do it when he had a gun and a chance of getting out. But he couldn't do it. He had to trust her, and do what she said, even if it meant swallowing his pride to keep on the good side of Barger as she said.

When he did drop off to sleep, all the fatigue and tension that he had been under for hours finally caught up with him, and he slept like a drugged man. When he woke, the first red gleam of sunrise was coming through the window. He sat up, rubbing his bristly face, and put his feet on the floor.

He reached for his shirt, yawning, and, when he failed to find it, he looked down. It was gone. So were his pants and boots and gun belt. He sat there, paralyzed. Even his hat and socks were gone. Nothing was left but his underclothes that he had on.

He looked under the bed, but the light was too thin to be sure they were not there. He crawled under the bed and felt around with his hands. Nothing! He looked in the corners of the room; he yanked the drawers out of the bureau and slammed them back. Empty!

He sat down on the bed again. Why? There was no sense to this. If he was to look for the money, he had to have clothes. But maybe Barger didn't want him to look. He couldn't ride without pants and boots. He couldn't fight without his gun.

He was a prisoner as much as Honey. Probably more. . . .
Then a terrible thought struck him. Honey had taken his
clothes. That was why she had come into his room during the
middle of the night, but she had found him awake, so she had
left. If he had been asleep, she would have taken his clothes
then. She must have come back later.

No, he was wrong. Why would she want his clothes? She
had no reason to hold him here as a prisoner, no more reason
than Barger. Still the suspicion lingered. He realized that, no
matter how much he wanted to free himself from the doubts
Grace Doane had planted in his mind about Honey, he had
failed.

He heard boots pound up the stairs and along the hall. Ed
got up and started toward the door. All he had were his fists.
If it was Barger. . . .

"Honey."

Barger's voice, but it was not the friendly tone of the night
before. High and shrill, the voice of a thoroughly angry man.
Ed put his hand on the knob and opened the door a crack.
Barger was out there. Riddle was behind him, standing beside
a squat man Ed had not seen before. Lance, perhaps, the man
Honey had mentioned.

Honey's door opened. She was still wearing her robe. She
asked: "What is it?"

"Did you get it out of him?" Barger demanded.

"No."

For a moment Ed wasn't sure what they were talking
about. She hadn't asked him anything that Barger wanted to
know. Then Barger began to curse. He gripped Honey by
both arms and shook her, shouting: "You wasted the whole
damn' night. You'd get him to tell you, you said. Use a little
sugar instead of vinegar. Now we've got to beat it out of him."

"You promised. . . ."

"If we got the map," Barger yelled, "but there wasn't any map. We went through his clothes. We'd have found it if he'd had one. Nothing. A couple hundred dollars in his pockets. That's all."

"You looked at his gun?"

"Sure. We even took the loads out of each shell. Nothing, I tell you."

"Might be on him," Riddle said. "Let's take a look."

"You don't have a pocket in your underclothes, do you?" Barger demanded. "We'll take a look, all right. With a quirt." He shook Honey again. "You god-damned floozy, you made a deal with him, didn't you? I'll let him go, and you two will hike out and get the money, and that's the last I'll ever see of you. I ought to beat hell out of you."

Honey cried out and tried to jerk free, but Barger slammed her against the wall, and held her there with one hand while he slapped her across the face with the other. Ed jerked the door open, yelling—"You son-of-a-bitch!"—and drove at Barger.

Surprised, Barger wheeled away from Honey, calling—"Riddle!"—but Riddle was too far away and too slow to stop him. Ed nailed Barger on the nose with a hard right; he felt the nose mash and saw the rush of blood, and swung his left. The blow never landed. Riddle slugged Ed on the side of the head with a roundhouse right that knocked Ed flat. Riddle jumped forward, a big boot swinging out, but Ed rolled and crawled with the frantic energy of an animal trying to escape from a bigger one, and Riddle's boot missed by inches.

Honey screamed: "You promised, Barger!"

Ed was on his feet now. He dived around Riddle, who was ponderously slow as he moved toward Ed, and then was on Barger again. He hammered him once in the belly, slashed a stinging fist high against the side of his head, and hit him in the belly again, doubling him over before Riddle caught Ed's arm and yanked him around and struck him on the cheek.

Ed was spun half around. He hit the wall, and his feet went out from under him. For an instant he could not move. His head was filled with a crazy ringing, but he was aware that Honey started toward him, and Barger struck her across the side of her face.

"Well, Lance," Riddle said, "looks like we've got a chore. Let's get to work."

Ed shook his head, trying to clear it, but the ringing was still there. He got up, backing away from Riddle and Lance, who were moving toward him. He ducked a fist that the squat man threw; he straightened and kicked Riddle in the crotch, doubling him over. Lance, driving in from the side, hit him in the ribs and then the neck and knocked him down.

Barger, holding a handkerchief to his bloody nose, said: "He's hell for punishment. Give him some more."

Ed was on his hands and knees. He glimpsed a pair of legs in front of him and grabbed. It was Barger. He brought the man down; he plunged forward, crab-like, and slammed his head hard against Barger's belly, driving the wind out of him, and then the ceiling fell on Ed.

Slowly Barger got to his feet and leaned against the wall, laboring for breath. Finally he said: "You didn't need to slug him, Lance, not with a gun. He's out cold. We can't get nothing out of a man who can't talk."

"He was tough to handle, boss," Lance said defensively. "Looked to me like it was time to finish him."

Riddle was straightening up, his face mirroring the agony that Ed's kick had sent knifing through him. He looked down at Ed as he said with grudging admiration: "A tough boy, boss. Real tough."

"A little like his brother," Lance said. "I recollect how Ben got Sandy and. . . ."

"Oh, shut up!" Barger bellowed. "This one isn't so tough. I'll shear the hair off his chest before I'm done."

"The first thing you know you'll kill him," Honey cried. "Then you'll never find the money. I won't forget you hit me, Barger. I've got a good memory."

He wheeled on her, his anger suddenly cooling. He said heavily: "I've got a good memory, too. Right now, I'm remembering you've lived here for four years, high and mighty with angel's wings popping out of your shoulders, but this bastard gets. . . ."

"You're wrong, Dal," she said. "Anyhow, it didn't seem very important to you as long as you thought I was going to get him to tell me where the money was."

"I can overlook a good deal for fifty thousand," Barger said. "I figured he might have destroyed the map, and that's apparently what he did. You didn't do your part, if you're telling the truth."

"I'm telling the truth, all right," she said bitterly, a hand feeling of her bruised mouth. "I thought I was saving his life, but he'll never understand. He'll hate me as long as he lives."

"No man hates you for very long if he's alive," Barger said, "and the dead ones don't count." He nodded at Riddle. "I'm going to the cow camp. Carry Morgan back into his room. He'll get a chance to talk when I get back tonight."

Honey looked at Barger, wanting him to see in her face how much she hated him. She said in a low voice: "There was only one thing I ever liked about you, Barger. You've always kept your word to me. You promised that, if I helped you, you wouldn't kill him."

He dabbed at his bloody nose, his gaze locked with hers.

"After living here for four years, you don't really know me, do you?"

"I guess not," she said. "I should have killed you the night you found Ben in the alley and brought him up to your room."

"Sure, that was your mistake." He turned to Riddle. "Talk to Morgan when he comes around. It'll be easier on everybody if you can get him to talk before evening. I won't be very patient when I get back. Tell him that."

Barger stomped down the stairs. Riddle and Lance carried Ed into his room and laid him on the bed. Lance went down the stairs, hurrying to catch up with Barger, but Riddle paused when Honey said: "Lou."

"Well?" he grinned at her. "You're licked, and you know it. You've played hard to get for four years, but now you're licked."

"Where's Gowdy?"

"Dal sent him out to see if Nason had gone. He won't do you no good, so don't count on him."

Riddle left her standing in the hall, a hand still touching her bruised mouth, and then she began to cry.

# Chapter Nine

Ed had the weird impression he was swimming upward through black water. His head ached with regular, pulsating explosions of pain that threatened to tear his skull apart. He began to turn back and forth on the bed, reaching out with his hands so that he could swim faster. Suddenly the blackness was not so complete. There seemed to be layers of it alternating with layers of light, and then he was aware that someone was holding his hands. He heard a familiar voice. "Easy, Ed, easy."

He pulled a hand free and felt of his thumping head.

Honey was bending over him, still holding one hand while she kept on talking reassuringly. "You're all right, Ed. You're all right."

Her face was quite close to his. Slowly his mind cleared. He was in bed, bright sunshine pouring through the window, and then he saw that one side of her mouth was bruised and swollen. He remembered. His clothes and gun gone, his fight with Barger and his men, and the sickening suspicion that Honey had sold him out to Dal Barger.

He jerked his other hand from hers. He muttered: "Sure, I'm all right. I had hell beaten out of me, but I'm all right."

She straightened up. "I'm sorry, Ed. I'm terribly sorry."

He tried to sit up. The room began to spin, and the hammering in his head was worse. He dropped back, groaning. "You're sorry. I'll bet you're so sorry you won't be able to sleep tonight."

"I don't expect to."

Another memory broke through the chaos of his thoughts, of Barger slamming Honey against the wall and holding her there when he slapped her, and later, when she had tried to

99

come to him, Barger had struck her again. He closed his eyes, wondering about it. Barger would not have beaten her if she had been playing his game.

When he opened his eyes, he saw that Honey had drawn a chair up to the bed and sat down. He asked: "Why did Barger hit you?"

"I was supposed to get you to tell me where the money's hidden, but I . . . I . . . well, I couldn't make myself ask that. I thought he'd find the map."

"Why couldn't you ask me where the money is?"

"There's no use talking about it." She rose and stood looking at him, her face reflecting the worry that was in her. "You won't believe anything I say."

Now he saw that one side of her face was bruised, too. It didn't make any sense. No sense at all. There could be little doubt about what she had tried to do. If he hadn't destroyed the map, Barger would have it now and be on his way to get the money. Still, she hadn't done enough to satisfy Barger.

"You came in and got my clothes and took them to Barger, didn't you?"

She nodded.

He said: "I don't savvy."

She walked to the window and stood looking down into the yard, the sunlight cutting sharply across her face. She was wearing a plain house dress that was faded to a dirty gray-blue, but sick as he was, Ed was struck by her beauty. Hers was a beauty that did not depend upon clothes or rouge or the way her hair was fixed; it was a part of her, a natural quality she did not have to struggle to attain as most women did.

"I'll get you out of the house some way, Ed," she said. "I don't know how, but I will."

"Where's my clothes?"

"You don't have any. They tore them up last night trying

to find the map, but your boots and gun belt are all right. They're downstairs."

"Get 'em for me. Or I'll get 'em, if you tell me where they are."

She shook her head. "Barger and Lance rode off this morning, but Riddle's downstairs. He'll kill you, if you start anything." She kept staring out the window as if trying to think of something to do.

He asked: "Where's Gowdy?"

"He's gone, too, I guess. Riddle's the only one in the house except the cook."

He thought of what Rufe Nason had said about her and Gowdy. Now, half believing it, he blurted, "What's Gowdy to you?"

She swung to face him, her hands clenched at her sides. "Nothing. I suppose you hate me. I suppose you want to believe everything you've heard about me that's bad. You'd feel better if you could hate me, wouldn't you?"

"Yeah, I'd feel better," he muttered. "I wouldn't be here if it weren't for you."

"I know. I asked you not to hate me, but. . . ." She turned away. "Talking's no good, Ed. It wasn't any good with Ben when he was in prison. I . . . I guess I don't bring a man anything but trouble."

He sat up and swung his feet to the floor. He propped himself upright with his hands on both sides of him, clenching his teeth against the agony that swept through him. Then it eased somewhat. He'd be all right in time, but time was something he didn't have. Barger would be back with Lance and Gowdy. They'd work on him until he told them where the money was, and then they'd kill him.

"If I'd stayed home where I belonged, I wouldn't be in this jam," he said bitterly. "I never thought a man was lucky when his troubles were just nursing cows and raising a little hay and hoping to hell he'd have enough money in the fall to pay his taxes and buy enough grub to get through the winter."

She was standing at the window again, her back to him. "I've heard Ben say the same thing. He wanted to go back, when I first met him, but his pride kept him from it."

"I suppose I'm to blame for that."

"Partly. I am, too, I guess. He wanted something better than hard work and poverty for me, and I was too young then to know what was important and what wasn't."

"Hell, you've got everything here."

"I don't want anything, Ed, not anything." She swung around to face him. "I've been nothing but an ornament for Barger. You've been told that."

He looked at her, wondering what he could believe. He had no way to distinguish truth from the lies he had heard since he had come to Gateway House. "Wouldn't be much satisfaction for Barger," he said finally, "just having an ornament."

"I earned my pay," she said quickly. "He's worked hard at what he calls building his political fences. He's brought important men here and taken them hunting. That's when I've been valuable to him, a hostess to sit at the table and, well, just talk and smile and be pleasant."

She could be telling the truth, he thought. She'd had to live somewhere, she'd told him, and Barger had given her a home while she waited for Ben. Four years. Maybe it was the truth and maybe not. He'd believe her when she got him out of here.

"What are you going to do about me?" he demanded.

"I don't know yet. I'll bring your dinner after a while. Maybe I can do something with Riddle. You stay here."

She left the room, shutting the door behind her. He rose

and took one step. Dizziness struck him again. He put a hand against the wall and held himself upright, pain beating through his head again. He closed his eyes, knowing that the only way to lick this was to stay on his feet. He got as far as the window and clutched the casing. Outside, the sunshine lay upon the red dirt of the yard with brittle sharpness, its glare hurting his eyes.

He lurched to the bureau, gripping it with one hand while he poured water from the pitcher into the bowl. He sloshed it over his battered face and went back to the bed and sat down again. To remain here until Barger got back was suicide, but tackling Riddle with his bare fists was an even quicker way to commit suicide.

He got up and walked around the room, feeling better. He thought of breaking up a chair and using a leg for a club, and then gave the idea up. Later, maybe, if Honey could get him close enough to Riddle to slug him. But would she? He had no good reason to trust her. It must have been that way with Ben, Ed thought, but his feeling was stronger than Ben's, so much stronger that, even if he got away, he knew he'd come back for her.

The sun was noon high. Ed walked to the door and opened it. He stood there, listening, but no sound came to him. He moved along the hall, making a quick search of all the rooms except Honey's. The hope had been in him that he would find a gun, or clothes he could wear, but the rooms were like his, just a little cheap furniture. Apparently Barger's room was downstairs.

He had returned to the hall when he heard someone coming up the stairs. He ducked back into one of the rooms, then he heard Riddle shout: "Morgan!"

No sense trying to hide. He stepped into the hall. Riddle stood at the head of the stairs, a gun in his hand. When he saw

Ed, he said: "Thought I heard something up here. What the hell have you been up to?"

"Looking for some clothes."

"You're wasting your time, bucko. Get back where you belong."

"I go back and wait for Barger. That it?"

"That's it," Riddle said. "I told you I had some dirty chores to do. Watching you is one of 'em. Getting tiresome sitting on my rump. You start looking around again and I'll entertain myself fixing you so you'll stay put."

"Don't anybody live in these rooms?"

"Just the Travers girl." Riddle laughed shortly. "If you're looking for clothes, why don't you try one of her dresses?"

Ed moved along the wall and stopped in front of his room. He said: "When I find Ben's money, I'll be in shape to pay good for any help I get."

"Save your wind," Riddle said testily. "I seen a man who double-crossed Barger. Wasn't pretty. Now get into your room and stay there. You hear?"

Ed had no real hope he could do anything with Riddle. Shrugging, he went into his room and sat down on the bed. He had left the door open, and presently he heard Riddle stomp back down the stairs. Nothing to do but wait like a condemned man in the death house.

He had no illusions about being a hero. He was a two-bit rancher with more ambition than was good for him. Dreams, just dreams. If he ever got back to the Laramie, he'd be satisfied to go on working his tail off just to keep himself in eating money. The showdown with Barger would come in a few hours. Ed wondered if he could find enough courage to resist the man. They'd use every Apache trick in the book to make him tell where the money was hidden. It would be easier to tell them and get it over with. Then a streak of perverseness struck him, when he thought of the way Barger had tried to double-cross Ben. To hell with Barger. He'd never get that money.

Honey came in with a tray of food, and he saw at once that she was angry. She said: "You couldn't stay here like I told you, could you?"

He said—"No."—and took the tray and began to eat. He was hungrier than he had realized.

Honey sat down on the chair. "You didn't do any good, and it made Riddle mad. He's hoping you'll get the idea of tying some blankets together and going out through a window."

"It'd be better than sitting here."

"You'd just give Riddle an excuse to shoot you." She frowned, her hands moving nervously on her lap. "If there had been anything in these rooms to help you, I'd have told you."

"Don't you have a gun?"

"No. I don't even have a knife, but I found a bottle of whisky. I'll try to get Riddle drunk before Barger gets back. I can't think of anything else to do."

He went on eating, doubting that it would work. If Riddle had a weakness for either whisky or women, Barger would not have left him alone on guard. He asked: "Why is Barger so hell-bent on getting this *dinero?*"

"It's partly a matter of pride because he didn't get the money from Ben. The rest of it's greed. After all, fifty thousand is quite a bit." Suddenly restless, she rose and walked to the window. "He has a fortune deposited in Denver banks. He's courting a society woman, but she won't come here to live, so he'll have to go to Denver. If he can sell Fishhook, he'll leave the country. He's got an Eastern syndicate interested now."

"How'd he make his money?"

"Partly from Fishhook. It's a good ranch. And gambling. He's even hidden outlaws for a price and helped them get across the line into Utah."

She had brought him a sack of Durham, a package of cigarette papers, and some matches. He rolled a smoke, his eyes on her. He could tell nothing from her face. She was reserved; the sense of intimacy that had been between them was gone.

"I suppose he hasn't married you because of the woman in Denver," Ed said.

"It takes two to make a marriage," she said curtly. "Or didn't you ever think of that?"

"Yeah, I've thought of it."

"He asked me to marry him when Ben went to prison. When I wouldn't, he hired me for a housekeeper." She picked up the tray and stood, looking down at him. "Ben sent for you, and you came. Why?" She swallowed, letting her face show the misery that was in her. "I'll tell you. You loved him. I loved him, too. I loved him enough to wait. I don't care what he thought about me or what he said to you. I waited. If you weren't his brother . . . oh, what's the use?"

She whirled and walked out, heels tapping sharply on the floor. He finished his smoke and rolled another, ashamed of his lack of faith in her. Again he was caught in that mental tug-of-war that had pulled him in opposite directions since the first time he had seen her in Gateway House. What he wanted to believe about her was contradicted by what he had heard from Ben and Grace Doane and Rufe Nason.

He rose and walked around the room. Perhaps Ben had been wrong about her. A man in prison could not see things fairly. Ben knew she had been living here on Fishhook in Dal Barger's house, so it was natural for him to think the worst of her, especially after getting Grace Doane's letters. Still he had loved her.

Ed turned to the window, a new thought occurring to him. Honey had been young when Ben had gone to prison. Since then she'd had four years to think about him and her future. A long time for a beautiful woman, wasted years. She could have gone away. Or she could have married Barger. So what she had said about waiting for Ben must be true.

He straightened, his thoughts running dry. Barger was riding in with Spur Gowdy and Lance. A moment later they disappeared around the corner of the house. They would probably rack their horses and come in.

Ed left the room and walked slowly along the hall toward the stairs, uncertain what he should do, or whether there was anything he could. He stopped, hearing the front door slam, then the jingle of spurs as men came in, and Barger's angry voice: "Lou, where did you get that bottle?"

"She brought it," Riddle said defensively. "I don't know where she got it."

"Go upstairs, Honey," Barger said in a flat voice. "Get into your room and stay there. I ought to take a blacksnake to you."

"Dal, I. . . ."

"Go on!" Barger yelled. "I'm not blind, and I'm not stupid. You figured on getting Riddle drunk so you and Morgan could make a run for it. You damned double-crossing bitch."

Ed stepped back out of the hall. He heard Honey's steps on the stairs, then she hurried past him into her room, and slammed and locked the door. She hadn't even glanced at him. He'd got her into trouble, and there was nothing he could do, and nothing she could do for him.

He heard the run of talk from downstairs, low-voiced, and

then Barger shouted: "The one thing I won't stand for is drinking when you're on a job! You know that."

"I had one drink," Riddle said. "That's all."

"You'd have had a hell of a lot more if I hadn't got back. She'd have fixed you so you wouldn't have known straight up from down, and we'd have lost both of them. I ought to take your hide right off your back."

"He's a good man for some jobs, Dal," Gowdy broke in. "No damage done."

"I never failed to do what I was told to do," Riddle said. "You're got no call to rawhide me over what I was gonna do and didn't. If you hadn't brought that woman here in the first place. . . ."

"All right, Lou," Gowdy said. "Let's see what Morgan's got to say for himself."

Ed moved back to the window and stood there, his hands on the sill behind him, panic threatening to overpower him. The waiting was over.

# Chapter Ten

They came in, Barger in front, his black eyes wicked with anger. Ed said: "So we're going through this again."

"No." Barger stepped ten feet from him and drew his gun. "We're not going through anything. All you've got to do is to tell me where the *dinero* is."

Barger wasn't the smooth, confident man he had been the night before. He wore the same dark suit, he held himself with the same austere dignity, but somehow he failed to give the impression of dominating strength that he had given the previous evening. Today he was just an angry man intent on finding out where fifty thousand dollars was hidden.

Ed laughed. For some reason the panic was gone. He'd licked Barger, in spirit at least, for now he sensed the man's weakness. Until he told where the money was buried, he held the ace that would keep him alive.

"You had me fooled last night, Barger," Ed said, "with your fine gab, but I've got you pegged now. When you get right down to cases, you're not much of a man. If you were, you'd tell your boys to leave and we'd settle this ourselves. Guns, fists, anything you want."

"He's offering you a deal, Dal," Gowdy murmured.

Gowdy stood beside the bureau, smiling blandly. He was the tougher of the four of them, Ed thought, and he had little respect for Barger. Barger was clearly afraid of him.

Lance and Riddle stood beside Barger. Riddle's face was dark with the sullen anger that Barger's rawhiding had aroused in him. Lance was not very bright, Ed judged. He had both strength and a compelling sense of blind loyalty, but Riddle was smarter, and he had a man's pride. There was, it seemed to Ed, a slim chance that Riddle could be detached from Barger.

"He didn't offer a deal," Barger said after a moment's silence. "What are you driving at, Gowdy?"

"How about it, Morgan?" Gowdy asked. "It struck me you made an offer."

"Sure I did," Ed said quickly. "Before you got back I tried to outbid you with Riddle, but he turned me down. Loyalty is hard to buy, Barger. It's a mistake for a man like Riddle to take what he took from you just now when. . . ."

"If you've got a deal in mind," Barger snapped, "let's have it."

"You heard me a while ago," Ed said. "You've got a lot of front. You fool most people, but you don't fool Gowdy. He takes your *dinero,* and all the time he knows he's a better man than you are."

Barger motioned with his gun. "I'm short on patience, Morgan. I want to know where the money is. If he's going to be stubborn, Riddle, you and Lance will have to persuade him."

"Wait," Gowdy said. "What he was saying was mighty interesting to me."

"Get your boys out of here," Ed said. "I offered to settle this between us, Barger. If I win, I walk out of here a free man. If you win, I'll tell you what you want to know."

"What about Honey?" Gowdy pressed.

"If I win, she goes with me," Ed said.

Barger's face was brick red. With Gowdy's help, Ed had boxed him in a corner, and it was plain that Barger realized what had happened, that he had been made to look bad before his men. He said harshly: "We've had enough gab. Get it out of him, Riddle."

But Riddle was slow to move, his anger still in him. He

said: "He made you a fair offer, Dal. Why ain't you taking him up on it?"

"Damn it, you're fired," Barger said in a voice that trembled with emotion. "Lance, go to work on him."

Lance laughed softly as he shuffled past Barger toward Ed. "I'll handle him different this time, boss," he said. "You watch me."

Ed judged that Barger wouldn't use his gun, not wanting to run the risk of killing the only man who knew where the money was hidden, and there was a possibility that Gowdy and Riddle would stay out of it, not a good chance as odds went, but the best bet Ed had. He drove at Lance, cracking him solidly on the face, and knew at once his gamble had failed. Riddle, prompted by years of habit, moved in from the side.

Ed wheeled, slashing Riddle in the belly, but that gave Lance an opening. The squat man got his big arms around Ed's waist and, lifting him off the floor, slammed him against the wall.

Ed's head struck the wall hard. He sprawled on the floor, and Lance fell on him, hammering him in the face. Gowdy said: "Easy, Lance, easy."

"Get off," Barger said. "Maybe he'll talk now."

Ed got to his feet, knowing he couldn't take much of this. He had been too badly hurt that morning. He stepped toward Barger, the man an indistinct shape before him. He said thickly: "I'll talk. I'll tell you what Nason said about you. Said you couldn't hold your woman. Said he'd seen Gowdy and Honey. . . ."

Barger shouted an incoherent oath, his self-control gone. He yelled: "Shut up. Shut the fuck up." He would have shot Ed, if Gowdy hadn't batted his gun barrel to one side, the bullet ripping into the wall.

"A dead man won't talk this side of hell," Gowdy said. "You came close to throwing fifty thousand dollars down a rat hole."

Barger jammed his gun into holster. He lunged at Ed, right fist swinging upward, and Ed, ducking, dived at the man. Riddle brought a big fist down in a brutal blow that struck Ed at the base of the neck. He fell against Barger and sprawled on the floor, knocked cold.

"You fool!" Gowdy shouted. "You can break a man's neck that way."

"Not his," Riddle said.

Barger dug a toe into Ed's ribs. "God damn it, can't we handle him without knocking him out?" Barger glared at Riddle, and then he seemed to sense the brooding anger that was still in him. "All right, Lou, we'll wait." He swung to Gowdy. "So it's common talk about you and Honey. Even Nason knew. . . ."

"I wouldn't say that," Gowdy broke in. "You're proddy because you haven't got anywhere with her in four years. Well, neither have I."

Barger stalked past Gowdy and went into the hall. He called: "Honey!" When there was no answer, he turned the knob of her door. Finding it locked, he kicked at it. "Open up, or I'll break the door in."

"I wouldn't, Dal," Gowdy said. "There's some things even I won't stand for."

Barger wheeled, humiliated and furious because Ed had showed his men what he was. He said in a low voice: "You're fired, Gowdy."

"Like Riddle?" Gowdy laughed shortly. "I think not. You've needed my gun in the past, and you're still going to need it."

Riddle and Lance had come out of the bedroom and were

watching uncertainly. Barger's gaze touched their faces briefly, then swung to Gowdy's. "All right, maybe I will."

"You know," Gowdy said, "Morgan's a real smart boy. He sure had you pegged. You'd better forget Honey and take a ride to Gateway House. You've got the Doane woman."

"Lance, stay downstairs," Barger said. "Riddle, you stay in the bunkhouse. Morgan will come out of it pretty soon. If he tries anything, tie him up. Maybe you'd better tie him anyway."

"He won't go anywhere," Gowdy said.

"See that he doesn't," Barger snapped, and stomped down the stairs and out of the house.

Gowdy motioned to Riddle. "Put my horse away when you take care of yours."

Lance went downstairs, but Riddle hesitated, still gripped by the anger that Barger had aroused in him. He began: "Put your own horse. . . ."

"Lou," Gowdy said softly.

Riddle swung away. Gowdy watched him, smiling, until the man left the house, the fear that he had stirred in Riddle bringing him a heady satisfaction. Then the smile left his lips as he turned to Honey's door. He called: "Barger's gone, Honey. Open the door."

The lock clicked, and the door swung open. Honey had been crying, finding relief at last from the tension that had been in her for so many hours. She leaned against the jamb, fighting for self-control, and then she asked: "Where did Barger go?"

"To a woman who appreciates him." He scowled, his eyes on Honey, then he said bitterly: "Hell of a thing for a man like me to work for Dal Barger. You thought he'd keep his word about letting Morgan go, if we found the map, but he wouldn't have. He don't aim to let you go, neither. He'd have

113

busted into your room a minute ago if it hadn't been for me."

"Thanks, Spur," she said.

She did not understand this pale-eyed, apparently guileless man who talked to Dal Barger in a way that no one else could. Gowdy had treated her with courteous deference from the first day she had come to Fishhook, and, although he had never said so before, she had instinctively sensed that Gowdy had kept Barger from forcing himself upon her. She had been alone with Gowdy many times, but he had never touched her; he had never said or done anything that made her think he loved her, yet she was sure he did.

He rolled a cigarette, the scowl leaving his face. He said thoughtfully: "You're a lot of woman, Honey. Nobody else could wear that rag of a dress and still be beautiful. Nobody else would have spent four years waiting for a convict to get out of the pen, either."

"Spur. . . ."

"I've got some talking to do," he said. "This is a good time for it. I've got a bellyful of Barger. Hell, what does he amount to? Got here at the right time when the country was empty, made some money, and fetches the big guns out here and acts so damned righteous it makes me sick. All the time he'd cut your throat for a nickel in cash money. Or mine, too. And I've been helping him make his splash while all I get is a piddling hundred dollars a month."

For the first time since she had known him he was letting her see the bitterness that had been fostering in him for so long. She watched him light his cigarette, sensing that he would help her and Ed Morgan, but not sure she could pay the price he would ask. She felt trapped and utterly helpless, wondering how this man who seemed so innocuous could be so deadly.

Gowdy jerked a hand toward Ed's room. "I'm jealous of

him. I was jealous of Ben. So was Barger. Well, I suppose you think you're in love with Morgan. I know you well enough to be damned sure it's the only thing that would make you stand up for him."

She nodded. "He reminds me so much of Ben, I guess."

"Maybe it's that. Might be something else, too. He's not like the riffraff you've been around for four years. He's got guts, and he's smart. Got his hooks into Barger a while ago. It was fun watching him." Gowdy shrugged. "Well, he won't be any good to either one of us if Barger tries again. We'll have to get him out of here tonight."

"You'll help?" she asked eagerly.

He held his answer a moment as if considering it. "I like the notion of having fifty thousand dollars without having to rob a bank to get it."

"Give me a gun. Ed could. . . ."

"That's not the way. Lance is downstairs. You can't handle him. Riddle's in the bunkhouse. Me, I'll be around somewhere. I'll saddle Morgan's buckskin and take a ride, then I'll leave him in front of the house." He looked at her through a drifting cloud of cigarette smoke, his pale eyes faintly speculative. "There's one catch."

So he was going to ask a price just as she had known he would. She breathed: "What is it, Spur?"

"You're not going with him. You'll be safe here as long as I'm around. If he balks, tell him you're afraid of meeting Barger on the trail between here and Gateway House."

She took a long, ragged breath, knowing this was not all he would ask, that he hadn't stated his full price. He would wait until Ed was free and she was beholden to him. But it was the only chance Ed had. Knowing the devil of fury that possessed Barger at times, she was certain that Ed would not survive another beating unless he talked, and then he was sure to die.

115

"All right," she said. "I'll stay."

He dropped the cigarette stub to the floor and stepped on it, a little smile on his lips. "Fifty thousand is enough to corrupt all of us, isn't it?"

"I wish I'd never heard of it!" she cried.

"You're not very practical, Honey. Fifty thousand dollars can buy you a lot of things. Tell Morgan to wait till sundown."

He turned and went down the stairs. She stood in the doorway of her room, listening. She heard him say: "Morgan won't give you any trouble, Lance, but just in case he does, remember he's not worth a damn to Barger if he's dead."

"Sure, Spur," the squat man said. "Maybe I'll go up and find out what the boss wants to know."

"You'll wait for Barger," Gowdy said.

Honey stood motionless until she heard the front door close. Then she crossed the hall to Ed's room. He was sitting up, his back against the wall, his eyes still glazed. She knelt beside him. "Ed! What did they do to you this time?"

He looked at her as if he didn't recognize her, and for a moment she was afraid he wouldn't be able to leave tonight. She shook his arm gently. "Ed, I'll help you get over to the bed."

She rose and, taking his hands, braced herself and pulled. He got to his feet and staggered across the room, Honey holding to one arm. He sprawled face down on the bed and lay still.

"Ed, can you hear me?"

He didn't move. She went into her room and came back with a towel. She soaked it in the water that was in the wash bowl, and then came to the bed and rubbed his hands and the back of his neck. She got him over on his back, and washed his face. His eyes had cleared, and she knew that he recognized her.

"They damned near finished me that time," he said hoarsely. "Next time they will."

"There won't be a next time," she said. "You're getting away this evening before Barger gets back."

"I'll have to crawl," he said.

"No, you'll have your horse."

"My neck hurts," he muttered.

"I'll get some liniment," she said, and went downstairs.

Lance was sprawled on the couch, a half-smoked cigar tucked in one corner of his mouth. She smiled at him as she hurried past, and he sat up, his slow mind nagged by suspicion. A moment later she returned with a bottle of liniment, and Lance rose.

"What have you got?" he demanded.

"Liniment. Morgan says his neck hurts."

Lance laughed. "It ought to, the way Lou hit him."

She went up the stairs, wondering how she could handle Lance. Ed was sitting up when she came into his room, his chin tipped down against his chest. He said: "I sure can't think straight. I got a hell of a wallop."

"Lie down," she ordered. "On your stomach."

She doused his back with the liniment and massaged him between his shoulder blades, then worked up to his neck, her hands moving with deft strength. He cringed as the liniment stung his skin, his hands knotted on the blankets beside him. Presently he said: "That's enough."

She rose, and put the cork in the bottle. "It's two or three hours till sundown. Then you're leaving, if I can figure out what to do about Lance."

Ed sat up again, turning his head one way, and then the other. "Good for man and beast, I reckon. Feels better anyhow."

"Did you hear me, Ed?"

"Yeah, I heard. Fetch him up here. I'll rap him on the head when he comes through the door. It ain't Lance I'm worried about. It's Riddle and that damned slick Gowdy."

"And just what will you use to rap Lance on the head with?"

He got up and put a hand against the wall, grinning wryly. "Feels like I've been through this before." Apparently the dizziness passed, for he reeled across the room to the chair, grabbed the back of it, and laying it on its side, brought a foot down sharply across a leg. It broke free, and he stooped and picked it up, then waved it in his hand.

"This'll do," he said, and lurched back to the bed.

"Lie down," she said sharply.

He obeyed, giving her a wry grin. "I'm stout," he said. "Just like a day-old calf."

"You'll manage when the time comes." She sat down on the side of the bed. "Ed, when you get away, go to Gateway House, and wait for me."

"You're leaving when I do."

"I can't. Barger's gone to Gateway House. I don't want to meet him. He's mad because I tried to get Riddle drunk."

"What's he doing at Gateway House?"

"Seeing Grace Doane."

Ed raised himself up on an elbow. "You trying to tell me . . . ?"

"Of course," she said impatiently. "Grace has been his woman ever since her father died. He won't marry her, though. That's why she hates him."

"I thought she'd shoot him on sight the way she talked."

"Hating and loving are pretty close together sometimes," she said moodily.

She remembered how it had been with Ben. They used to

118

quarrel until she was sure she hated him and he hated her, yet they had always made up, and then it was sweeter for the quarreling. Now, looking at Ed's battered face, she thought how much like Ben he was and still entirely different. The violence that had so often showed itself in Ben did not seem to be a part of Ed.

"I'll get away from here as soon as I can," she said. "You wait for me at Gateway House. Let's forget about the money."

His face was stubborn then, his bruised lips down-curved. She had seen that same expression on Ben's face many times. She could guess how it had been between them when Ben had left home. Both stubborn, neither willing to give an inch, with Ed finally forcing Ben to give way because he was younger. That was why he had left. Now she wondered how it would have worked out if Ben had gone back home.

"I'll get that *dinero*," Ed said. "I'll get Barger, too. Didn't seem to make much difference one way or the other when I first got to Gateway House, but it does now." He ran a tongue over puffy lips. "I don't like the idea of leaving you here."

"I'll be all right," she said. "Gowdy will see to that." She saw suspicion cloud his face, and she added quickly: "Barger's afraid of him."

"I saw that this afternoon. Well, he's gonna be afraid of me before I'm done."

"You'd better try to sleep," she said. "I'll wake you."

He nodded, and reached for her hand. "I'm coming back for you. Don't you forget it."

"It's the one thing I don't want to forget," she said, and left the room.

When she went back downstairs, she saw Lance straighten up and watch her with close attention. She put the liniment away and returned to the living room and sat down on the couch beside Lance. She said: "Morgan's in bad shape. I don't think he can stand another beating."

His opaque eyes were fixed on her. He said accusingly: "You ain't fooling me. You're on his side."

She slid closer, so that her right thigh pressed against his left one. She said: "I'm on his side because he's the only one who knows where the money's hidden. If Dal kills him, none of us will get it. Isn't that right?"

He was stirred by her presence, but he was a cautious man, too, fully aware of what Gowdy would do to him if he laid a hand on her. He edged away as he said: "You had your chance last night to find out where the money was."

"I thought Dal would find the map." She leaned forward and laid a hand on his left leg. "Listen, Lance. Dal wants that money. Now, if you and me could get Morgan to tell us where it is, Dal would like it, wouldn't he?"

Suspicion still clouded his mind. He said: "You was trying to get Riddle drunk when we came in. You're a double-crossing bitch."

She rose. "You aren't very smart, Lance. You've got a chance to do something that will make Dal think a lot of you, but you're turning it down."

She started toward the stairs. He said: "How do you figure to make Morgan talk?"

Turning, Honey looked at him gravely. "I know how badly he's hurt. I'll tell him he's got till sundown. I think that will be enough to make him talk, but if it isn't, you won't have to do much to get it out of him. He'll be worrying about it from now till sundown."

Lance frowned, laboriously thinking about this. He said finally: "Won't hurt nothing, I reckon. Dal would like it fine if I got it out of Morgan for him." He scratched his fat nose, the desire to please Barger balanced against his suspicion of

Honey. "What's it gonna get you?"

"If I help you, Dal will owe me something, won't he?"

"Yeah, reckon he will. All right. You tell Morgan he's got till sundown."

She smiled. "That's fine, Lance," she said, and went up the stairs.

She looked in on Ed and thought he was asleep. She went into her room and lay down, closing her eyes. She was sick with the misery of regret. If only she could have looked ahead, she would never have come to Fishhook. She could have found some kind of work in Canon City. She could have seen Ben often, and he would have trusted her if she had been there. But now it was too late to do anything for Ben. Saving Ed's life was the only thing that counted. If Gowdy double-crossed her, she would kill him. She didn't know how, but she'd find a way.

# Chapter Eleven

Ed did not intend to sleep, but Honey had relaxed his neck and shoulder muscles. He dropped off, and he stirred once, vaguely aware that Honey stood in the doorway, and then he slept again. When he woke, the sun was down and twilight had moved in across the mesa.

He sat up stiffly, his body aching in a dozen places, but he wasn't dizzy, and his mind was working with sharp clarity. Whatever he did must be done now. He rose and kicked the broken remains of the chair under the bed. He crossed to the bureau and washed his face in the tepid water in the basin, wondering where Honey had gone. She must have heard him, for she crossed the hall to his room.

"How do you feel?" she asked.

"Better'n I expected." He turned to the bed and picked up the chair leg. "I'll go down and see Lance."

"Stay here," she said sharply. "I'll fetch him upstairs like you said."

He didn't remember saying that. He didn't remember anything very clearly after he'd come around except that Honey had rubbed him with liniment. He was keyed up and nervous, and it seemed that he couldn't wait. He might get killed, but he wasn't waiting.

"I'm going down. . . ."

"I said to stay here. Right here by the door." She motioned to the place where she wanted him to stand. "I'll get Lance."

She was gone then, and there was nothing to do but obey. It began coming back to him, slowly, Honey's saying that Barger had gone to Grace Doane, that she was staying here but he was to wait for her at Gateway House, and that he'd have his horse. He didn't understand, but he had to trust her.

122

Riddle was around somewhere. Probably Gowdy. They'd cut him down before he could get to the corral.

Lance and Honey were coming up the stairs. He gripped the chair leg in his right hand, crowding against the wall. He heard Honey say: "You won't have to get rough, Lance. Just tell him what you're going to do to him."

"You're sure he's ready to cave?"

"I'm sure. He's had all he can stand. You promise to let him go and he'll talk."

They stopped just outside the door. There was absolute silence for a moment, and Ed had a terrible fear that Lance wasn't coming in. Then the man said: "I don't see him. Must be hiding in a corner."

"What's the matter with you?" Honey demanded. "You've got a gun, and he's been beaten up till he can't stand."

"I don't see him," Lance said doggedly. "If he can't stand, where is he?"

"He's on the bed. Close to the wall."

"You've got better eyes'n I have," Lance muttered.

"Give me your gun if you're afraid of him," Honey said contemptuously. "I'll make him talk."

"I ain't afraid," Lance snapped, and stepped into the room.

Ed gripped the chair leg tightly. He held it high, and, the instant Lance appeared, he swung. The club made a sharp crack as it struck Lance's head. There was no necessity for a second blow. The squat man's knees buckled; he spilled forward and fell as soddenly as a dropped sack of wheat.

"Hurry," Honey cried. "Your gun belt and boots are in the living room by the table. Your horse is saddled and tied to the hitch rack in front of the house. Take Lance's shirt and pants."

She snatched up Lance's gun. Ed removed the man's shirt and pants and put them on. He asked: "Who saddled my horse?"

"Gowdy."

The shirt was too big, the pants too short in the crotch and legs, but they'd do. He asked: "Where does Gowdy stand in this deal?"

"He won't stop you. It's Riddle you'll have to watch out for."

"You're going with me. My horse will carry double."

"I told you I had to stay!" she cried. "I'll be safe here."

He remembered, but he didn't like it. He said: "Barger will kill you for helping me get away."

"No, he won't. I'll tell him I couldn't stop you. How would I know what you'd do to Lance?"

There was no time to argue with her. She was right. Barger wouldn't harm her. If Ed did run into the man on his way to Gateway House and there was a fight, Honey would be in more danger than if she stayed here. Still, it went against his grain to leave her, and he stood motionless, caught in a trap of indecision.

She gripped his arm. "I know how you feel, but I'll be all right, Ed. Wait for me at Gateway House."

"I tell you I'm coming back," he said. "I've got something to settle with Barger."

"That's how Ben got caught," she said. "It's not revenge that's important. Saving your life is."

He kissed her, and then she clung to him, her face against his chest. He said: "Maybe Gateway House isn't the best place to wait. Not if Grace is Barger's woman."

"Go on to Montrose, then." She stepped back, still holding Lance's gun. "Don't worry about me. Barger won't know I've got this gun. He'll think you took it. I'll use it, if I

124

have to, and I'll find you, Ed." She gave him a push toward the stairs. "Go on now."

He went into the hall, then looked back at her, tall and proud and beautiful. Ben had been wrong about her, he thought. If he never saw her again, his life would be empty and worthless. He couldn't go off and leave her. He'd get his gun and stay and fight.

She must have sensed his thoughts, for she cried out: "Ed, you can't be a fool now! I've done this much for you. I can't do any more."

"But I can't go off and leave. . . ."

"Go on!" She was almost hysterical. "I made a deal with Gowdy. That's why I've got to stay. Now will you go?"

It would have been the same if she had struck him across the face. She might as well have told him she never wanted to see him again, that she belonged to Gowdy. Wheeling, he went down the stairs, fighting the dizziness that swept over him. Honey and Spur Gowdy! So Rufe Nason had been right, after all. To hell with her. To hell with all of it. He'd save his neck while he could.

He found his boots and pulled them on; he buckled his gun belt around him and checked the gun. The loops of his belt were empty, but the cylinder held five shells. He opened the door and looked out. The dusk light was strong enough for him to see his buckskin tied to the hitch pole. Riddle was around somewhere, but, if Ed could reach his horse, he had a chance.

He lunged through the door and sprinted across the yard. He yanked the reins away from the pole and hit the saddle, then he heard Riddle's great yell and pulled his gun from his holster. Riddle was coming across the yard from the bunkhouse, and he fired, the bullet slicing through the front of Ed's baggy shirt.

125

Ed dug steel into his buckskin's flanks and, turning, pulled his trigger. The hammer fell, but there was no explosion. He was nailed. A gun with five empty shells and Riddle throwing down for another shot. Why hadn't he taken Lance's gun instead of leaving it with Honey?

The buckskin lined out in a run. Ed heard a shot, but he wasn't hit, and, when he looked back, he saw it was not Riddle who had fired. The man was down in the dust of the yard. The shot had come from the corner of the barn. Gowdy! Honey had made a deal with him for Ed Morgan's life.

He couldn't go back. Gowdy had kept his part of the bargain. Honey would be all right. Ed pulled his horse down to a walk, his head aching again. He clutched the saddle horn, afraid for a time that he was going to faint, but he never quite lost consciousness. A few minutes later he was out of the valley that held the Fishhook buildings, the last trace of the sunset fading in the west.

Every step the buckskin took sent pain knifing through Ed. He rode with his head down, one hand still gripping the horn. Presently he revived enough to realize he was not on the road that led to Gateway House. He swung to his left, found the road, and headed his horse along it, realizing that, if he met Barger, he was a dead man. An empty belt and an empty gun! Even if he didn't run into Barger, what would Grace Doane do when he showed up at Gateway House? He couldn't stay there. Maybe he could get past and go on to Montrose.

The next hours were torture with only one idea flogging his pain-numbed mind: he had to keep going. It was completely dark now, but the sky was clear and filled with stars. The road ran on endlessly across the grass, and time flowed by, seemingly as endless as the road before him. Then he was aware of the piñons, crowding against him like two black walls, and he knew he was close to the Cañon of the Diablo.

126

Nothing was quite right or quite real. There was a nightmarish quality about everything. He started down into the cañon, the vast sea of empty space to his left. He gripped the saddle horn so tightly that his hand ached. For some crazy reason he had a desire to jump off into the cañon, to drop and drop until he had left everything behind him. Honey and Gowdy! She had given Ed his chance for life. But he had to go back. Later! Much later when he could fight. Now he was a wounded animal crawling toward his hole to hide.

Then Ruth was in his mind again, his wife who had given him his one fine year. But she was dead. And Ben who had sent for him was gone, too. Honey had said he loved Ben or he wouldn't have come. She was right. But Ben had given him a job. He'd go back. He'd go back. It was a refrain that kept running through his feverish mind and would not stop.

Ben had loved Honey, and now Ed loved Honey, and he had to go back for her. That was the way Ruth would want it, for she was gone, and Honey was alive and Honey belonged to him. She loved him or she wouldn't have made a deal with Gowdy. Maybe she loved him because he reminded her of Ben. But he was Ed, not Ben. Did Honey know that, or was she still thinking of Ben?

He was down beside the river; he heard the taunting whisper of it as it ran toward the Dolores, a river filled with life and movement. But he was alive, too. He had to live to go back to Honey. The barn at Gateway House loomed before him, and the buckskin went on around the corner to the front and stopped in the yawning doorway, the lantern overhead a murky point of light in a pressing pool of blackness. His hand relaxed from the horn, and he spilled out of the saddle and the ground came up and hammered at him, shocking him back to consciousness.

Hamp came to him. He cried out—"Morgan!"—and knelt

beside him. "What the hell happened to you? Your face looks like you tangled with a grizzly."

"Barger," Ed breathed.

"That son-of-a-bitch," Hamp whispered. "That stinking son-of-a-bitch. He's here."

Ed couldn't move. He looked up at the old man's face that seemed to be close and then faded away and came close again. Suddenly Hamp rose and led the buckskin into the barn. He returned a moment later and knelt beside Ed again.

"Listen, Morgan," Hamp said. "Can you hear me?"

"I can hear you," Ed said. "Seems like I can't move."

"You've got to. Barger will be out here any minute now. He'll kill you if he finds you." When Ed didn't say anything, Hamp went on. "You've got a gun. Get it out of the holster and shoot the bastard."

"Empty," Ed said.

Hamp swore. "I don't have a gun out here, and I can't go into the house after one. You've got to move. Understand? You've got to get inside. I'll throw hay over you, and maybe he won't see you. Come on, now. I ain't spry enough to lug you inside."

Ed could move. He got up on his hands and knees and began to crawl, his head hammering again with those thundering spasms of pain that seemed to tear his skull apart. "Keep going," Hamp said. "Keep going, or I'll get a pitchfork and ram it into your behind!"

Ed got through the door and went flat again, his face nose-deep in the barn litter. Hamp swore and, getting him by an arm, tugged at him. Ed made another effort. He crawled on his belly, Hamp pulling at him, and then Hamp said: "All right. He's coming. I heard a door slam. Now be still. If he spots your horse, you're a dead duck."

Hamp crawled over a manger and frantically forked hay

into the stall. Ed heard low voices, and presently he recognized them. Barger's and Grace Doane's. Hamp crawled back over the manger, moved some of the hay until Ed was completely hidden, and leaned the fork against the side of the stall.

Barger came into the barn. "Saddle my horse, Hamp."

"There's your horse and there's your saddle," the old man snapped. "To hell with you."

"Hamp," Grace said sharply.

"I'm not taking orders from him!" Hamp shouted. "You tell me to saddle his horse and I'll do it."

"You'll do it . . . ," Barger began hotly.

"Saddle up for him," Grace cut in.

The old man moved out of the stall and went back along the runway. Barger said: "That old fool needs a lesson."

"Not from you," Grace said. "I'm done with you, Dal. Don't come back."

He laughed indolently. "I'll be back, and you'll be the same. You belong to me, Grace. Don't fight it."

"But you don't belong to me," she said bitterly. "I'm damned tired of it being a one-way proposition. Go back to your Honey Travers."

"Maybe I do belong to you," Barger said. "I'm about ready to move to Denver. I'll get that fifty thousand all right, and I've got a good prospect who'll buy me out. When you've got enough money, you can go anywhere and do anything."

"You'll move to Denver, but I'll still be here," she said disgustedly. "Don't lie to me."

Hamp returned with Barger's horse. "Get the hell out of here," Hamp said. "If you come back again, I'll kill you."

Barger struck Hamp and knocked him flat on his back into the barn litter. "Don't talk to me that way, old man." He swung into the saddle. "So long, Grace."

"It's good bye," she said. "You made a mistake, just now."

He laughed arrogantly. "You'll never change," he said. "I'll be back." He rode away. Grace did not move until the sound of his horse had died on the road.

Hamp sat up, feeling of his jaw. He said: "Well?"

"You're right about him, Hamp," Grace said. "But he's right, too. I'll hate him as long as he's gone, but when he comes back, it will be the same again. I can't help it."

Hamp got up and leaned against the wall, still feeling of his jaw. He said: "Then we'll get out, all of us. That devil's hurt you enough."

"Hamp, Hamp," she breathed. "You know I can't go. I've got you and Billy and Lissa to look after. Maybe Dal will leave, and then it'll be all right again."

"Would twenty-five thousand of Morgan's money be enough to get you to go?" the old man demanded. "We could buy another hotel. It's what you've always wanted."

"Sure, sure," she jeered. "Why not take the whole fifty thousand? All we've got to do is to find it if Dal doesn't find it first."

"He won't," Hamp said.

"But he will. He's got Morgan."

"Has Morgan told him?"

"No. That's why Dal was so ugly. They knocked Morgan out twice, but he can't go on holding out. No man can."

"Take a look over here," Hamp said.

He walked into the stall where Ed lay and kicked the hay off him. "Morgan, you can get up now."

There was no answer. Grace cried out and ran to him. "When did he get here?"

"A little while before you came in with Barger." Hamp felt of Ed's wrist. "He's alive. You look after him, and maybe he'll be all right. He'll make the deal you want this time, or I miss my guess."

She stood looking down at Ed, her mouth a tight, bitter line across her face. She whispered: "Is there anything good in Dal, Hamp?"

"You never found any, did you?" the old man asked sourly.

"There used to be," she said. "I think there was a time when he really loved me."

Hamp swore. "Well, he don't now. That's sure. He don't love nobody but himself. Go get Billy up. We'll tote Morgan into the house, and you're gonna nurse him. We'll get the *dinero*, and I'm hoping we'll fill Barger full of lead while we're doing it."

131

# Chapter Twelve

The next three days were one as far as Ed was concerned. He slept most of the time, or lay with his eyes closed, every movement he made sending spasms of pain through him. Grace would come in and, lifting his head, shove some pillows under it; she would spoon soup into his mouth and talk softly to him. He said very little, and what he did say was an incoherent jumble except when he called for Honey.

Grace was never far from him, and now and then Hamp came in. The third day the old man said: "You've got to give him time. Hard to tell how much. If he's got a concussion, well, it's just hard to tell."

"Maybe he'll never be all right," Grace said worriedly. "Or if he is, he may not remember where the money is."

"He'll come around. He's a tough *hombre,* or he'd never have got here. Looks like Ben, don't he?"

"Acts like him, too. Must have been a tough family."

"Reckon so. Well, he's got to have rest. Pretty soon he'll figure out he's safe and with friends, and then he'll be all right."

Ed heard them, but he gave no indication that he did. He was not sure how he'd got here. The last memory he had was of hearing Barger's voice and of Hamp, throwing hay on him. He knew he was in Grace's room and wondered where she was sleeping, then he thought of Honey, and he began to fret about her.

Hamp's words—"She's safe and with friends."—were the best medicine he could have had. He had no worry about himself. All he wanted was time to get back on his feet. He told himself that Honey would be all right. She had a gun, and Gowdy would look out for her.

He dropped off to sleep again. The next morning, when Grace came into the room, he was sitting up. He looked at her, grinning a little. "Thanks for looking out for me," he said.

She dropped into a chair as if her knees had given way under her. She whispered: "Morgan! Are you all right?"

"I will be. I've got a hell of a lot to do."

She was close to crying from sheer relief. She said nothing for a moment, fighting back her tears, then she got up. "I'm getting soft," she said, "but I thought you were a goner. I'll get your breakfast. You lie down. No hurry about anything."

He lay back on the bed, knowing that this was something he could not lick today. Time! He swore softly, staring at the ceiling, his thoughts on Honey. And Gowdy. What sort of deal had she made with the gunman? Was it Honey he wanted? Or the money? Or both?

Grace brought him a breakfast of ham and eggs and coffee, and he ate with relish. She said: "It's good to see you eat, Morgan."

"Good cooking," he said.

"Feel like talking?"

"What about?"

"What did they do to you?"

"They thought I had a map," he answered. "When Barger didn't find it, he got ornery. Tried to beat it out of me."

"How'd you get away?"

"Gowdy helped me."

"Well, I'll be damned," the girl breathed. "So he's after the money, too. Ben didn't know what he started when he sent you here."

"He sure didn't." Ed felt of the back of his neck. "I'm sore as a boil. Have you got any liniment?"

"I'll find some," she said, and took the tray from him and left the room.

She returned presently with a bottle of evil-smelling stuff that was as strong as the liniment Honey had used. He lay on his stomach, and she massaged his back and neck, and, when she was done, she said: "Hamp and me looked you over, but we didn't find any broken bones. We were afraid you had a head injury."

"They slugged me with a gun barrel," he said. "Maybe I have."

"You'll have to take it easy," she said. "We'll have a hard time finding that money."

"We?"

"I'm not really a Good Samaritan," she said, tight-lipped. "My offer still holds."

"It's fair," he said dully, "but there's one thing you don't know. I'm going to kill Barger before I leave the country."

She turned without a word and walked out of the room. He had no doubt now that Honey had been right about Barger and Grace. After that, Barger was not mentioned for ten days. Ed found he was not as weak as he had thought he would be, now that he was able to eat. He took his meals at the table, Hamp usually eating with them. There was a cot in the kitchen. Grace had been sleeping on it, Ed judged, so she could be close to him.

Grace found some clothes that fitted him better than Lance's, and a battered Stetson. When he told her he needed shells, she brought him a box without questioning him. He filled the loops of his belt, checking the gun carefully, and then stepped out through the back door and emptied it at an aspen trunk. He was relieved when he discovered it had not been tampered with. He had carried it for a long time, and he was glad he did not have to ask for another one.

He was cleaning it when Hamp came in from the front of the house. The old man asked: "What's the shooting about?"

"Just finding out if my gun still worked." Ed glanced at the old man. "Haven't seen anything of Billy Lowe."

"He's busy," Hamp said evasively.

Ed let it drop, but he guessed that Lowe didn't like him. He wasn't sure that it made any difference unless Lowe favored Barger, and he doubted that. After Hamp left, Ed thought about it, and later in the day he asked Grace how Lowe felt about Barger.

"Like Hamp," she said shortly.

"Honey told me about you and Barger," Ed said.

She dropped into a chair across the table from him, her brown little hands knotted in front of her. For a moment she was silent, her dark eyes staring absently at the wall over his head. Then she asked: "What about it?"

"Didn't make sense, not after hearing you talk about Barger like you done."

"No, it doesn't make sense," she agreed. "I couldn't explain it, not even if it was any of your business."

"Maybe it is my business," he said. "You know what'll happen when we go after that money. If you think so damned much of Barger. . . ."

"I don't." She hammered the table with a clenched fist. "I wouldn't raise a finger to save his ornery hide." She got up and walked to a window. "Morgan, you're a man. You couldn't understand how a woman felt."

"Maybe I could," he said quietly.

She swung to face him, her hands on her slim hips. "No you wouldn't. I wasn't lying when I told you he just thinks about himself. He's wanted Honey from the first, and he's never had her. It makes him crazy, but sooner or later he comes to me." She swallowed. "When he's not here, I hate him, but when he is, I'm like a piece of soft putty. I can't help myself, Morgan. I'm ashamed, but it's the way I am."

"You talked about Honey as if. . . ."

"I lied about her." She came back to the table and sat down, her face quite pale. "I hate her because she's prettier than I am." She shook her head. "No, that isn't really it. I know I'm second choice with Barger. Honey hired out as his housekeeper and that's all she has been."

"Gowdy?"

"How would I know about men?" she cried. "There's talk, but maybe talk doesn't mean anything. We're like a bunch of old women when it comes to gossip." She rose and began walking nervously around the room.

He smoked a cigarette, watching her. Finally he said: "I'll be ready to ride in a few days. I can sleep upstairs, and you can have your bed back."

"Tomorrow," she said absently, and then swung to face him. "When I was younger, I think Barger really loved me. I keep telling myself that, and I keep hoping. I'll never love another man." She laughed shortly. "That makes me a real smart woman, doesn't it, Morgan?"

"Why are you so bent on getting a hunk of that money?"

"I've told you," she said impatiently. "Hamp, Billy, and Lissa worked for my dad for years, and now they're old. I've got to look out for them. If I had the money, I'd leave here, and . . . and maybe I could forget Barger."

He did not know what he would do after the money had been found, but that was something that could be decided later. Honey had said she would come here, but she hadn't. Then suddenly a suspicion took shape in his mind.

"Have you heard or seen anything of Honey since I got here?" he asked.

"No," she answered quickly. "I wouldn't lie to you about that, Morgan. When we first brought you here, you kept asking for her. Hamp thought we ought to try to get her, but I knew we couldn't, so I didn't try."

He believed her. He was jealous of Gowdy, but there was the balancing knowledge in his mind that Honey had made it possible for him to get away from Fishhook. Whatever deal she had made with Gowdy must have been made only because she loved him, not Gowdy. When he reached that point in his thinking, he was sick with regret for having left her at Fishhook. The old refrain began running through his mind again. He had to go back.

"Maybe we ought to start tonight," he said.

"No. We'll wait."

She left the room. She was hoping Barger would return, he thought, hoping that by some miracle things would be right between them again. But they never would, not if he understood Barger, and he was sure he did.

The next day Ed moved upstairs to the room he'd had the first night he'd been here. He did not see either Billy Lowe or Lissa, and Grace told him to stay in the room. She brought his supper that evening, and he sensed at once she was excited about something.

When she returned for his tray, she said: "Barger will be here tonight. No matter what happens, you stay in this room."

"I want Barger," he said quietly. "Why wait?"

"You can't kill him here," she cried. "I don't want to be anywhere around when it happens."

She left, slamming the door behind her. He couldn't trust her, he thought bitterly. If it came to a showdown, she would do what she could for Barger, and all of her talk about loving Hamp and the others and wanting to look out for them wouldn't mean anything. He examined his gun, dropped it into the holster, and made his draw. He shook his head. Slow. Too slow. Against a killer like Gowdy, he would have no chance at all, but Barger wasn't Gowdy.

He heard the door open and swung around. Billy Lowe came in, a double-barreled shotgun held on the ready. The old man said in a cold, wicked voice: "Morgan, Grace don't want you beefed, but I ain't above doing it if you don't toe the mark."

Hamp was a kindly man, but Billy Lowe had a mean streak in him. Staring at him now, Ed wondered what his presence meant. Lowe's faded eyes were on him, waiting for him to make a hostile move, his craggy face bitter.

"You don't like me, do you?" Ed asked.

"Not a little bit," Lowe said. "I don't cotton to a hairpin like you who shows up pretending he's somebody he ain't. Your brother Ben was straight, but I ain't sure you wouldn't steal the pennies off a dead man's eyes."

"Thanks," Ed murmured. "What's the scatter-gun for?"

"To see you stay here. Grace is bound and determined to go after that *dinero,* so me and Hamp will string along, but you ain't busting things open while Barger's here."

"You favor Barger?"

"Hell, no. All he's ever done is to make Grace miserable, but one of his men showed up a couple of hours ago, and he'll probably have some more of 'em with him when he rides in. This ain't no time for a showdown."

Ed moved to the window and stood looking into the yard. It was dusk now, and he could see Hamp's stooped figure come from the corrals and disappear into the barn. Ed asked: "How do you figure Grace and Barger ?"

"None of your business."

"I've got my hide to look after. I figure it is my business."

Lowe took a long breath. "Yeah, maybe it is at that. Well, I figure he's got her hypnotized. Don't make sense no other way. She's a good girl except when it comes to that bastard.

I'm just praying I'll live long enough to see him dead." He pulled a chair to the door and sat down. "Take it easy, Morgan. You're gonna be here for a while."

Ed said nothing. He remained at the window, and presently he saw three men ride around the barn and come on across the yard. They racked their horses at the hitch pole and went into the house. Ed said: "They're here."

"How many?"

"Three of 'em."

"That's what I figured. He's fetched his boys down from the high country. He'll let his cows go to hell if he figures he's got a chance to get his hands on you."

"Think he knows I'm here?"

"He might. He's a smart huckleberry, and by this time he's pretty damned sure you ain't on the mesa."

There were no freighters at Gateway House tonight, just a few miners on their way to Sentinel. The dusk light grew steadily thinner, and presently it was dark. Ed could hear the racket from the bar. His head was throbbing again, and he realized that his nerves had tightened up.

If he could get his hands on Barger! In the darkness he might get the drop on Lowe, but he'd have to kill the old man, and he wouldn't do that. It was the one thing that would unquestionably turn Grace and Hamp against him. He wouldn't get out of the house alive anyhow, not with Barger and three of his men here. But he had to know about Honey.

He swung around. "Lowe, I'll stop here, but I'm about crazy worrying over Honey. You go down and find out what's happened at Fishhook."

"You are crazy if you're worrying about Honey Travers," Lowe snapped. "Don't know nothing that balls a man up in his thinking like being in love. Same with a woman. If it wasn't for Barger, Grace would be. . . ."

"Lowe," Ed said ominously, "I want to know about Honey."

"I ain't budging," the old man said. "Grace, she said to keep you here till Barger leaves, and, by damn, that's what I'm gonna do."

Ed turned to the window again, standing so that his right side was against the wall. He knew Lowe's position; he could pull his gun and whirl and shoot the old man, and then he'd be free to go downstairs. He couldn't do it, but still the temptation haunted him. As the minutes passed, the tension built in him until it was unbearable. He was caught with the devil's own choice, not wanting to lose this chance to kill Barger and at the same time knowing the man was out of his reach.

Lowe's chair scraped against the floor, and Ed turned, his back pressed against the wall. The old man opened the door, and lamplight from the hall made a pale splash on the floor. Lowe said: "Ain't no trouble to figure out what you're thinking, mister, but if you plugged me and went downstairs, you'd be a gone goose. If you had any savvy, you'd know that."

Horses left the yard in a sudden drum of hoofs. Ed wheeled to the window and looked out, but in the darkness he could not see how many men had left. Presently the sound of their departure died on the narrow road beyond the barn. Someone was running up the stairs, and, when Ed turned, he saw that Grace had come into the room. She lighted a lamp and stood looking at him, breathing hard, two spots of bright color on her cheeks.

"I was afraid you'd do something foolish, Morgan," she said.

"He wanted to, damn him," Lowe muttered. "He's as easy to read as a book."

"We're pulling out tonight," Grace said. "Barger's gone

140

with his men. He's had his crew combing the mesa for you, and he can't figure out what happened to you."

"You figure he made a good guess?" Lowe asked.

"I couldn't tell," she answered, "but I'm afraid he'll put one of his men to watching the place. Hamp's got our grub packed up, so we can get away in a few minutes. Help him saddle the horses, Billy."

Lowe hesitated, his head tipped forward, malevolent eyes on Ed. "You trusting this huckleberry, Grace?"

"I've got to!" she cried. "I can't stay here any longer."

Lowe took a deep breath. "I dunno who's the biggest fool, but it must be me 'n' Hamp. We'll get killed, all of us. I've got a feeling."

"Just like your rheumatism tells you it's going to rain," she jeered. "Go on now. Fetch the horses to the back door."

Swearing softly, Lowe left the room. Ed moved toward the girl, sensing something had happened that had erased the last slim hope she held. He asked: "What is it, Grace?"

She looked up at him, a new boldness in her eyes, her high-pointed breasts rising and falling with her breathing. "Nothing except what I knew would happen. I just didn't want to believe it would come. Barger's got a letter making an offer for his holdings. He'll be gone in a few days, and I'll never see him again. He'll go to Denver and marry a woman who's right for him. He'll forget me, and I'll forget him."

He asked: "Do you think you can?"

"You're damned right I can. I hate him. I never hated anybody like I hate Dal Barger. It's kind of funny, so funny I'll laugh about it someday." She gave him a wry grin. "You and me are in the same boat. We've been left at the gate, so I guess we belong together. You're more man than Barger ever was, and, if you give me a chance, I'll show how much woman I am."

She was making an effort to be subtle. He could have her for the asking, a single word, a gesture. Then the full significance of what she had said hit him with the numbing impact of a physical blow. He gripped her arms. "What about Honey? You know, don't you?"

"Sure I know." She jerked her arms free and lifted her hands to the side of his face. "You and me, Morgan. We've got each other and nobody else. We'd better take what we can when we can. No sense counting on someone else who lies to you and cheats you, is there?"

"What about Honey?" he demanded. "Are you going to tell me . . . ?"

"Sure I'll tell you." She whirled away and stepped to the door. "Come on. Blow out the lamp."

"Don't fool with me now!" he shouted at her. "You tell me . . . !"

"I'm not fooling." She looked back over her shoulder, a brittle smile on her lips. "Honey ran away with Gowdy. Barger doesn't know where they are, and he's mad as hell. Served him right. Served you right for believing her. Well, I'm here, and she's not. Come on. We'll be riding in a few minutes."

He blew out the lamp and followed her down the stairs. He was much too shocked to think coherently. Honey had promised to come to Gateway House, but, instead, she had run off with Gowdy. So it had been more than talk. She had got rid of him so she could have Gowdy. It was all right, if that was the way she wanted it, he told himself. It was all right.

# Chapter Thirteen

The moon was up when they left Gateway House, Hamp taking the lead. Billy Lowe was in the rear, leading a pack horse. To Ed's surprise, they headed up the Diablo, following a narrow ledge above the river, a brawling stream that was silver-coated by the moonlight. Ed did not ask any questions, for he had been cautioned by Hamp not to talk. He didn't feel like talking anyhow, not now after knowing about Honey.

A few days before Ed would have said it was impossible to love and hate a woman at the same time, but that was the way it was. He had believed she'd made a deal with Gowdy to save his life. Now he knew he had believed it because he had hoped it was true. If Grace had told the truth, and he did not doubt that she had, he could not escape the conclusion that Honey had got rid of him so his death would not be upon her conscience, and then she had left with Gowdy.

Ben had called her a bitch because he knew her, and that made Ed a credulous fool. That was what hurt. No matter what she did or where she went, he would never forget the sweetness of her lips. It must have been that way with Ben.

About half a mile east of Gateway House they reached a small stream that tumbled down the side of the south wall of Diablo Cañon, which was not as steep at this point as it was at Gateway House. Hamp left the river and turned up the creek, hoofs making a loud clatter on the gravel bottom. Ed understood now what Hamp had in mind. Barger would expect them to follow the road until they reached the mesa, so he would station a man up there to watch them. This way, if they were lucky, they could reach the south rim before Barger knew they had left Gateway House.

Several times Hamp had to leave the stream and circle

deep pools, then make a stiff climb to get above rapids or falls, but he always returned to the creek. It was hard going, and they paused often to rest their horses, moonlight filtering faintly through the pines, the rumble of the creek the only sound in the silence.

Once when they were stopped, Grace told Ed: "We're gambling Barger doesn't know about getting out of the cañon this way."

"Plenty of time to talk later," Hamp said curtly. "We don't want to run into an ambush."

A foolish precaution, Ed thought. Horses couldn't go up a rocky slant like this without making racket that could be heard farther than Grace's voice would carry. They went on again, the creek following a slit in the side of the cañon so narrow that it was hardly wide enough for a horse.

Ed had no idea of the time it took to get on the rim. He wanted a cigarette, but he knew what Hamp and Billy Lowe would say if he struck a match. It didn't make much difference, he thought dully. Nothing made much difference now, but he didn't light a cigarette. He didn't feel like arguing.

Then the walls that had hemmed them in from the time they had left the Diablo fell away, and they were on top. Hamp swung west from the creek to follow a game trail through the piñons, and presently he pulled up in a small clearing.

"We'll stay here today," he said.

Dawn was a thin, gray promise in the east, but there was still some time before the sun would be up. "Why don't we travel till daylight?" Ed asked.

"I want to see if Barger sends a man back to Gateway House," Hamp said. "There's a point of rock yonder one of us can watch from. Besides, his crew are hunting for you on the mesa. I don't want to run into 'em."

They swung down, Billy Lowe taking care of the horses. Ed had no way of being sure, but he judged they were not far from the eastern edge of the mesa. Hamp was clearly in command, and that suited Ed. He trusted Hamp, but he wasn't sure of Lowe.

Hamp made a small fire of dry piñon limbs. While Grace cooked breakfast, the old man hunkered by the fire, his gnarled, liver-spotted hands spread over it. By the time they finished eating, the sun was showing above the San Juans.

"That's the last hot grub we'll have for a while," Hamp said, as he kicked the fire out. "We ain't making no smoke while it's daylight."

"I'll watch till noon," Lowe said. He picked up his Winchester and disappeared into the piñons.

"Who's going to run Gateway House?" Ed asked.

"Lissa," Grace said. "She'll get a fellow who lives across the river to do the chores."

"What happens when Barger finds out you're gone?"

"Hard to tell," Hamp said irritably. "We'll figure that out when the time comes." He picked up a piñon stick and began drawing a map in the dirt. "Morgan, we want to know where we're headed."

Ed had known this decision would be forced upon him sooner or later, a matter of trust that had to be decided. Grace was watching him closely, her small, dark face taut with anxiety.

"I don't know about Lowe," Ed said. "He may take a look at fifty thousand dollars and decide that's twice as much as twenty-five."

"I'll handle him," Grace said.

"You ain't dealing with Barger," Hamp said sharply. "If you don't trust us, we sure as hell ain't gonna trust you. The mesa's a big piece of country, and finding a couple of saddlebags buried somewhere on it is gonna be a chore."

"All right." Ed knelt beside the map Hamp had drawn. "Where's the falls on the Diablo?"

Hamp made a cross on the line that represented the river. "Here." He made another cross marking the location of Fishhook. "You've seen this part of the mesa, but Ben didn't leave his *dinero* around the falls or the ranch. I know where the posse caught him. Must have been around there."

"I spotted the falls," Ed said. "There was a notch on the divide south of it, and I saw a finger of rock on the south rim. I figure the *dinero*'s hidden on a line between the spire of rock and the north."

"I know that spire." Hamp marked its location on the south rim. " 'Bout there. Still a big piece of country, Morgan."

Hamp and Grace watched him, knowing he had more to go on than what he had said. "I destroyed the map Ben gave me," Ed said, "but he mentioned the rimrock was red with yellow streaks running through it."

"That isn't enough," Hamp muttered. "Damn it, man, I've lived in this country for years. I know it like the palm of my hand, know it as well as Barger does. There's a dozen places where the rimrock has yellow streaks."

"There were two pine trees close together," Ed said. "The money's buried between them."

Hamp rose and threw the stick down. "That all you know?"

"That's all."

The old man looked at Grace in disgust. "There's a thousand pine trees and a lot of 'em grow close together. No use even looking. Why, hell, that was four years ago. One of those pine trees might be down by now. Or both of 'em."

"We'll try," Grace said, tight-lipped.

Hamp picked up a blanket. "I'm gonna sleep till noon," he said, and disappeared into the piñons.

Ed did not meet the girl's eyes. He said: "We might as well get some sleep, too."

He lay down, his head on a saddle. She came to him and sat beside him. "Morgan, maybe this is a wild-goose chase. We don't have much to go on."

"It ain't as bad as Hamp's letting on," Ed said. "He don't like this business no better than Lowe does. They want to go back."

"Do you?"

"No."

She sat down beside him, an arm dropped across his body. "Morgan, you know how it could be with us. We've both lost what we want."

He knew, but there was a difference between them. She had lost what she had never really had, not if he pegged Dal Barger right. Now, lying there beside her with his eyes closed, he thought of Honey and how sure Ben had been that she would go with him when he came for her. Maybe Honey was still in the country; maybe Ed hadn't lost her, if he could find her again. Then he thought: *I'm as bad as Grace, hoping when there's nothing to hope for.*

He propped himself up on an elbow and, looking at her closely, saw the eagerness that was in her face. She didn't care for him. She never would, not the way he loved Honey or the way Grace had loved Barger. Hurt pride was prompting her. If she ever saw Barger again, she wanted to be able to tell him she had a man, a better man than Dal Barger ever was.

"It's no good, Grace," he said. "It wouldn't do."

She pulled her arm back and lay flat on her back. "It's still Honey, isn't it?"

"It'll always be Honey," he said.

147

Grace closed her eyes. She whispered: "Damn her. God damn her."

There was no more talk. They both slept, and were awakened when Hamp returned to the clearing. He took a canteen and some biscuits and jerky, and picked up his Winchester and disappeared into the piñons again.

"Hungry?" Grace asked, coolly indifferent now.

He nodded, and she brought him a canteen and a sack of biscuits and a handful of jerky. Presently Lowe appeared. He helped himself to the food and ate noisily, and, when he was done, he said: "A fellow came down the road about an hour ago, stayed at Gateway House a few minutes, and went back. I'm guessing he found out we're gone."

"Barger will be along," Grace said. "He'll track us, won't he?"

"That's the way I figure," Lowe said. "Well, we'll be all right till Hamp gets us moving. I'm gonna sleep. One of you better stay awake."

"I will," Ed said.

The sun was noon high, the heat dry and brittle even here in the shade of the piñons. Lowe lay down and was asleep at once. Ed rose. "Looks like we'll be riding all night. You'd better sleep while you can."

She smoothed her riding skirt over her knees, nodding absently. "I'd better fill the canteens," she said. "We might have to get away fast."

She gathered the canteens and walked toward the creek. Ed waited until she returned, and then he left the clearing, suddenly restless as he considered the possibility of some of Barger's riders finding them. It would be sheer luck, but it could happen.

He struck off through the close-growing piñons, moving silently, and found that the trees thinned out within fifty yards of the clearing. He stopped, eyes searching the open country that spilled away for miles to the south and west.

They were as he had guessed, on the extreme edge of the plateau. Foothills, thinly timbered, rose in steadily mounting tiers toward a rugged mountain range. From this point he could not pick out any landmarks that he knew. Neither the notch at the divide north of the Diablo nor the rock spire to the south was visible.

He sat down, fighting the desire to sleep again, his head aching with the dull throbs that had become almost as familiar to him as the beating of his heart. He smoked a cigarette, and put it out carefully, for the piñons were tinder dry. Then he stood up, suddenly tense. Two riders appeared over a rise of ground to the west.

He considered going back and waking Lowe, and decided against it because he wasn't sure whether the Fishhook men were simply looking, or if Barger had made a good guess. Then he breathed easier, for he saw the men were angling off to the south. They passed within a quarter of a mile from where Ed stood, screened by a piñon, and disappeared in a notch between two hills.

Ed sat down again. The afternoon wore on; he dozed occasionally and woke with a start, fighting the weariness that had been in him from the time he had left Fishhook. Impatient with his weakness, he wondered how long it would take him to get over the beatings he had taken at Fishhook.

He wasn't even sure it was the beatings that had taken the steam out of him. It might have been the lack of sleep and fatigue from the hard ride the night before. Or maybe it was the letdown from the tension that had gripped him from the moment he had received Ben's letter. Or perhaps it was none of those things.

In spite of anything he could do, Honey crawled back into

his mind again. Then, honest with himself, he admitted it was his sense of loss that forced this unfamiliar feeling of lassitude upon him. Finding the money and killing Barger would not compensate for that loss. Nothing could.

Near sundown he returned to the clearing. Hamp was there, silent and tight-lipped. They ate a cold supper, Lowe watered the horses, and, when it was dark, they mounted and rode out of the piñons, Hamp taking the lead as he had the night before.

Ed brought his buckskin up beside Grace. He asked in a low tone: "What's bothering Hamp?"

"Barger never showed up at Gateway House," Grace said. "Hamp can't figure it out. He thought the fellow who was there would fetch Barger, and they'd be on our tail before now."

"I saw a couple of men this afternoon," Ed said. "Just riding and looking, I guess. Think Hamp ought to know."

She shook her head. "He figures the mesa is crawling with Fishhook men. It wouldn't make any difference."

In a few minutes it was fully dark and the stars came out, and the dark line of the eastern hills was lost against a black sky. They were moving due south, taking the long way around, Ed saw, and remaining as far from Fishhook as they could. They rode down into an arroyo and came up out of it, crossed a level strip, and reached another arroyo, and went on that way for miles. There was no sound except for the thud of hoofs dropping into the grass and the howling of coyotes from the rim to the south.

A cool wind ran in across the flat, bringing with it the stirring incense of sage and piñon and cedar. A weird prickle ran down Ed's spine. He had the feeling he was being squeezed beneath the layers of earth and sky. He wanted to cry out, to make himself heard, to challenge anything that moved out here in this vast, empty land. He gripped his saddle horn, swearing softly as he fought his nerves.

Hamp pulled up, and they sat in silence, listening. Still no sound came in from the grass, no sound at all except the grunting of a horse or the faint squeal of leather as someone shifted his weight in the saddle. At this moment even the coyotes were silent.

They went on, and presently a round moon rolled up above the mountain crest, the pale light giving a distorted sense of proportion to the hills on one side and the plateau on the other that seemed to run on and on into infinity. Sometime after midnight they swung west, the country broken now by steep draws, and then they were threading their way between huge monoliths, tall, grotesque ghosts in the moonlight.

A wicked, barren country, Ed thought, and he wondered what it would look like in daylight. He wondered, too, how Ben had felt that day the posse had caught him. He was alone and hunted; he could not have been sure he would ever see Honey again, or whether he would use the money he had in his saddlebags. Barger who had double-crossed him was still alive, and there was nothing Ben could do but run. The anger that had burned hot and then smoldered in Ed now became a bright, hot flame again as he thought about Ben.

There was still no sign of dawn when Hamp drew up in a small, cup-like depression. He said: "We'll get some sleep. We ain't far from where you'll start looking."

Ed stepped down. He moved to Grace's horse and held up his arms to her. She almost fell out of the saddle. He caught her, and for a moment she leaned her head against his chest. Then she looked up at him, and he realized how utterly weary she was.

"It's not worth it," he said.

"It will be," she said, "if we find the money."

Lowe staked out the horses while Ed and Hamp gathered wood. They built a small fire, and Grace cooked a meal. While they were eating, Ed asked: "What'll we do for water?"

"There's a creek west of here," Hamp said, "but I figured we oughta look things over before we make camp."

"You figure Barger's beat us here?"

"He'll have some of the boys watching for us. You can bet your bottom dollar on that. Barger will guess mighty close to where we're going."

So that was why Barger had not tried to track them after they had left Gateway House, and it was why Hamp had been concerned when they hadn't. The old man had expected a fight in the piñons that had not come. If Barger were dead, they could quit worrying. This was worse; they didn't know where he was or when he would hit them.

They slept until the sun was well up. A hot day, Ed thought, with little shade, the searing heat intensified by the barren rock. They ate a cold meal, drinking sparingly from their canteens. Then, without a word, Lowe saddled his horse and left.

"Where's he going?" Ed asked.

Hamp lighted his pipe and moved to the slim shade of a tall rock. He held his answer for a time, faded eyes appraising Ed. He said: "We're in a hell of a shape in case you haven't figured it out. If Barger's got his men on the rim, they'll cut us down before we see where they are."

"Lowe's taking a look on the rim?"

Hamp nodded. "Runs along here for miles. There's plenty of places where they can hole up, but Billy will probably draw their fire, if they're up there. Leastwise we hope he will."

"How far have we got to go?"

"A mile or more. Hard to tell just where Ben came across

152

the mesa. It's my guess he aimed to go on south. Then, when his horse went lame, he probably got boogery and buried the *dinero* and started his run for the state line."

"You're making one bad guess the way I see it," Ed said. "Barger won't hit us till we find the money."

"I'm hoping it'll be that way," Hamp said grimly, "but you can't out-figure that ornery son-of-a-bitch. He might knock the rest of us over and take you alive."

"He won't," Ed said. "He'd never find out from me where Ben hid the money."

Grace gave Hamp a wry smile. "Barger knows that, after what they did to Ed, so he'll wait till we find it."

# Chapter Fourteen

Hamp refused to move until afternoon. "Billy was willing to make bullet bait out of himself," the old man said doggedly, "and I aim to see he gets time to do it."

Grace turned away, saying nothing. Ed wondered if she had any regrets, now that they had come this far. Billy Lowe had had a foreboding of death before they'd left Gateway House, but Grace had treated it lightly. If he were killed, she would never forgive herself, not if she was as loyal to the two old men as they were to her. Now Ed could not doubt Lowe's loyalty, as he had a few hours before.

The sun had swung westward when they left the cup-like depression where they had camped. They still held close to the base of the cliff. Staring upward at it, Ed understood what Hamp had meant when he had said there were a dozen places where the rock wall was streaked with yellow. In general, the cliff was the same dull red as the dirt underfoot as well as the innumerable boulders and spires and grotesque piles of slab rock scattered aimlessly along the south edge of the mesa, but here and there strata of buff and yellow broke the monotony of color. Still, it did not bother Ed, because they were looking for two pines, and here there were no trees except a few wind-shaped cedars.

There was no sign of Lowe on the rim, and they were too close to see the tall spire that Ed had mentally marked when he had located the falls and notch in the divide to the north. Looking across the mesa, Ed could see the divide, made small by distance, and then, quite suddenly, he located the notch. When he called Hamp's attention to it, the old man merely shrugged.

"Sure. I knew we could see it, and that spire you spotted

154

ain't far ahead, but don't forget Ben was on the run. He was scared, maybe too scared to think straight, so we can't be sure he was traveling due south from the falls like he thought he was."

An hour later the country leveled out, and they were among the pines. Here the red sod held a rich carpet of grass. Not far ahead a line of willows marked the creek that Hamp had mentioned. He pulled up suddenly, saying with satisfaction: "Looks all right. Billy's got a good pair of glasses, and he's had time to study things out."

Staring upward at the man, Ed saw Lowe standing close to the edge, swinging his hat. He was still some distance west of them. Hamp waved back, then glanced questioningly at Ed. "What do you think of this for a camping spot?"

Grace sat slackly in her saddle, plainly relieved now that she knew Lowe was all right. She said: "Looks good to me."

But Ed wasn't satisfied. He said: "We're too far from the creek. Them willows make a fair cover for a man. Every time we went down there, we'd be asking for a slug."

Hamp scratched a wrinkled cheek, frowning thoughtfully. For a long moment he was silent. Ed, looking out across the flat, saw that there were a number of rocky upthrusts within rifle range, red spires that had been eroded by countless centuries of wind until they assumed all sorts of fantastic shapes. All of them were tall enough to hide men and horses.

"Hard to tell which is the smart way to play this," Hamp said finally. "Maybe we oughta camp closer to the creek."

"This is too damned open to suit me," Ed said. "I'll take a sashay out yonder and see what's on the other side of them rocks. Why don't you and Grace go on to the creek. I'd feel better if we had some protection against a surprise."

Hamp nodded. "I was a little worried about them rocks yonder. Take it easy, boy. You might ride into a slug."

Ed nodded, and swung his buckskin north. He rode

warily, his gun held across his saddle horn, and two hours later returned to the base of the cliff. Hamp and Grace had dismounted and pulled saddles from their horses in a grassy area fifty yards from the creek. At this point a sandstone ridge jutted out from the cliff. It was a little higher than a man's head, good enough protection against an attack from the west. A few scattered boulders that had tumbled from the rim lay to the east.

"This suit you?" Hamp asked.

"Probably the best we can do." Ed jerked his hand northward. "Nobody out there. No sign that anybody's even been there lately."

He stepped down and off-saddled. Lowe was nowhere in sight, but there was a break in the rim above the sandstone ridge. A man could bring a horse through the break, although it was steep and cluttered with boulders. It was late afternoon now, and, when Ed returned from staking out his buckskin, Hamp had started a fire.

"Spot your two pines?" Hamp asked, grinning slyly. "Gonna walk right out there and start digging where Ben left the *dinero?*"

"It'll take some looking, maybe. You figure this is the place?"

Hamp nodded. "The spire you were talking about is a little to the southwest."

Ed smoked a cigarette while Grace cooked supper. The pines were scattered, most of them standing alone, but from where Ed stood he could see seven pairs of trees that might be the ones Ben had marked. More than that, he saw a windfall that had stood quite close to another pine. There was a possibility it had been standing when Ben had buried the money. Now Ed realized that Hamp had not understated the difficulty they faced.

"Come and get it!" Grace called.

Ed walked to the fire. "Lowe gonna eat?"

"He'll come down after a while." Hamp gave Ed a straight look. "Well, how about it?"

"It'll take luck," Ed admitted, and refused to give the old man any more satisfaction than that. "Time enough to start in the morning."

"Sure," Hamp murmured. "We've got all summer."

Lowe appeared presently, riding carefully down the steep slope. He ate in silence, avoiding Ed's gaze, and, when he was done, he threw his tin plate down. "No sign of nobody up there," he said, "but, hell's fire, there's plenty of places I can't see into." He glared at Grace. "Sure, I'll go back and I'll stay there, but I've got a feeling in my backbone I don't like."

"I've got the same feeling," Ed said quietly. "We're the men who'll find the *dinero,* so I figure we'll be the targets, not you."

"*If* you find it," Lowe grunted.

"I was wrong bringing you here," Grace said miserably. "Why don't you go back to Gateway House, Billy? You, too, Hamp?"

Lowe and Hamp looked at each other, grinning a little. Then Hamp said: "We've lived our lives. Don't make no difference, either way."

Lowe nodded agreement. "Reckon I've had enough of Gateway House," he said. He mounted and rode back to the rim.

They took turns staying awake that night, the last guard falling to Ed. He had awoken once, dreaming of Honey, but when he had reached for her, she had eluded him. He had tried to call to her, then Grace was shaking him, crying: "Morgan, what's the matter with you?"

He must have been talking in his sleep. He had sat up,

shivering, the illusion shattered. A dream? His life would be filled with dreams, dreams that would never be anything more than that. He had said: "Nothing. Go back to sleep."

Presently Hamp appeared and shook Ed's shoulder. "Your turn," he said, and, leaving his Winchester, moved on past Grace to his saddle and blankets.

Ed rose. He picked up the .30-30 and walked toward the creek. He shivered in the cold wind that moaned as it drove against the cliff and flowed through the pines, and he wondered how a country could be so perverse, hot by day and cold by night. He kept moving, listening to the night sounds, trying to sort out one that seemed unnatural, but there was none to alarm him.

The wildness of that land was in the rocks and the wind and the trees, a wildness that seemed to work into a man's bones. No one would ever change or tame a country like this. Again Ed was aware of the eerie, spine-tingling sensation he had felt the night before when they were riding. But there was a difference now that stemmed from the feeling he was being watched. Imagination, he thought, exaggerating the danger because finally they had reached the place where Ben had buried the money, and Hamp was sure Barger's men were not far away.

Ed thought of Ben and their boyhood together, of the mistakes he had made, and he wished he could live those years again. Then he thought of his wife Ruth, of Ben asking: "She was a good woman, wasn't she?" He owed her a great deal, for she had changed him, and Ben had sensed that change.

Now, alone with his thoughts, he admitted to himself that, although he had loved Ruth, she had never stirred him the way Honey did. No matter how this search for the money turned out, he would not go back to his ranch until he had found her. He would not be satisfied until she told him she did not love him, that it was Gowdy she wanted.

The opalescent light of dawn began edging up into the eastern sky, and he heard Grace moving about. He came in and started a fire, hunkering beside it as the flames leaped up from the dry pine limbs.

Grace was covertly watching him, but he said nothing to her. At the moment he didn't feel like talking. He knew that Grace would come to him if he'd let her, and afterward she'd leave him, if Barger gave her so much as a kind word. For some reason he could not understand, he was embittered by that thought. They were caught, all of them, trapped by past events, by great hungers, their lives twisted so they would never be the same again.

They let Hamp sleep, and presently Billy Lowe rode down from the rim, tired and sleepy and cranky. He was covered by red dust. The wind had blown harder up there on the rim than it had down here, Ed thought. Lowe wolfed his breakfast and, taking a canteen, rode to the creek and filled it and watered his horse.

He came back and reined up, looking down at Grace. "It's the damnedest country I ever saw. You can't see nothing and you can't hear nothing, but all the time you know you're being watched."

"I had the same feeling," Ed said.

"Well, find that damned *dinero* and let's get out of here," he said.

For three days Ed searched, Grace working with him most of the time, Hamp doing the camp chores, and Lowe watching from the rim. With each sundown the sense of failure weighed more heavily upon them. Using the shovel Hamp had brought, Ed dug between every pair of trees that seemed close enough to be the ones Ben had marked on the map, but he found nothing.

Ed was certain Ben would not have buried the money more then a foot or two deep, harassed as he was by the knowledge that he was on foot and a posse would appear any minute. Ed was certain, too, that Ben would have left the money directly between the trees, so there was no necessity to dig up a wide area.

Three days of back-breaking digging forced Ed to accept one of two conclusions: someone else had found the money, although that seemed unreasonable since there was no evidence of previous digging, or Ben had buried the money somewhere else, perhaps farther west.

He brought up the question the third night as they ate supper, but Hamp shook his head. "We'd have heard about it if the *dinero* had been found. You're wrong on the other count, too. The only pines on the south side of the mesa are right here. Cross the creek and you get the same kind of country we came through before we got here. Nothing but damned red rock."

They were silent then, Ed knowing that both Hamp and Lowe were anxious to call it off and start back. But Grace wasn't willing to give up. Presently she said: "There's that windfall, Ed. We haven't tried digging between its roots and the tree that's still standing."

"I've thought of that," Ed admitted, "but it looks like it's been down a long time."

"You can't tell," Hamp said. "Better give it a try in the morning. If you don't. . . ." His voice trailed off.

"We go back. That it?"

"That's it," the old man said defiantly. "This here's like living with ghosts staring at you all night. Enough to make a man go loco. We don't see nobody, but they're out yonder all right."

Every morning, before he started digging, Ed saddled his buckskin and made a wide circle to the north just as he had the first afternoon they had come, but he saw no evidence that anyone had been there. Now he rolled a smoke and lighted it with a burning twig, his eyes on Hamp's deeply lined face.

"I'm not sure anybody's watching us," Ed said. "When I stand guard, I get the feeling that someone's around, but I figure it's jumpy nerves. We're so damned sure Barger's gonna make a play for the money that we're seeing a pair of eyes behind every bush."

Grace had moved away from the fire. Hamp said in a low tone: "This morning I rode down the creek a piece. Plenty of fresh tracks in the mud. Jumpy nerves don't make tracks."

Ed poked at the fire, saying nothing. He didn't want to call Hamp a liar, but he had a strong feeling that either Hamp or Lowe would do anything to make him and Grace give up. He wouldn't believe the tracks were there until he saw them.

"Better be careful about riding down the creek," he said finally.

"I aim to be," Hamp said, "but the minute you find that *dinero*, the sky's gonna fall on us. Only now I'm thinking you won't find it. Ben didn't give you enough to go on."

"He should have marked the tree or something," Ed agreed, "but he was in too much of a hurry, and, when he talked to me, he knew he was dying, so all he could think of was to convince me I had to come."

Ed found it hard to sleep that night, knowing the old me were giving him only one more day. It seemed that he h; barely dropped off when Hamp woke him to stand guard. rose stiffly, every muscle crying out in protest. In three d

he had moved more dirt than he would ordinarily move in a year.

As he walked away from camp, he saw that a storm was coming. Thunder made an ominous rumble to the west, and lightning played along the horizon. He hoped the day would be cooler. Dawn came slowly that morning, for the sullen clouds had swept on across the sky to cover it, hiding the mountain peaks. A rain would add to the old men's cranky impatience, he thought sourly.

For some reason Hamp woke earlier than usual. He ate breakfast with Grace and Ed, and, when it was fully light, he picked up the canteens, saying: "I'll go get some water." He licked his cracked lips, glancing at Grace. "Billy and me talked it over yesterday. Come sundown, we're pulling out."

She said tonelessly: "All right, Hamp."

He patted her shoulder. "We'll make out. Hell, Gateway House ain't so bad."

He walked away, leaving Grace staring at the fire. Hamp didn't really understand, Ed thought. It wasn't just staying at Gateway House and trying to take in enough money to pay Barger's interest and taxes and buy supplies. Grace wanted to show Barger she wasn't bound to him, that she could go away and free herself from him. Her half of the money would let her do that.

"We'll try that windfall today," Ed said. "We've got till sundown. If you want to, we'll go back over every hole we've made and work down another foot or two."

"No use, Ed," she whispered. "All the time I knew we shouldn't do this, but I couldn't help it." She began to tremble. "Now I'm afraid. We've stayed too long."

Ed heard Hamp's terrified yell; he grabbed the old man's Winchester and whirled toward the creek as a gunshot hammered into the early-morning silence. He saw Hamp fall; he

glimpsed a man on a horse with a smoking gun in his hand. He brought the rifle to his shoulder as the rider whirled his horse and dug steel into the animal. Ed had one clear shot before the man disappeared behind the screen of willows, and he wasn't sure whether he had hit him or not.

Grace screamed and ran toward the creek. Billy Lowe brought his horse plunging down the boulder-strewn break in the rim at a reckless pace. Ed caught up with Grace and ran past her; he reached Hamp and knelt beside him. The old man was dead. The bullet had struck him in the chest.

Ed rose and caught the girl in his arms. "He's gone, Grace."

He held her while Lowe came on to them in a hard run. He yanked his horse to a stop and swung down; he took one look at Hamp and wheeled to Ed and Grace. "Dead. Murdered by some damned cowhand who didn't give a damn about this business one way or the other."

Grace was crying, her head against Ed's chest. Ed said: "That talk won't help any."

"You took a shot at him," Lowe shouted. "Did you get the bastard?"

"I ain't sure."

"If you missed, I'll come back and kill you!" Lowe bellowed. He stepped back into the saddle, rode across the creek. There was nothing Ed could say to Grace. He had liked and respected Hamp, a good man who had died because he was loyal to Grace, and Ed knew she was aware of that.

Lowe came back. "You got him," he said. "He hung on for about fifty feet and fell out of his saddle. He's dead."

Grace stepped back from Ed and lifted her face to Lowe. "Say it, Billy. I'm to blame. Say it."

"No use," Lowe muttered. "He's gone."

"We'll bury him beside Dad," Grace breathed.

"Bury him here," Lowe said, "and we'll do it now. Don't make no difference where a man's buried. That *hombre*'s horse will go back to Fishhook, and we'll have the lot of 'em on our necks."

Grace didn't argue. Ed packed up Hamp and carried his limp body from the creek. He laid him down in the grass and went back to the camp for the shovel. When he returned, he asked: "This the right place?"

"Good enough." Then Lowe did a surprising thing. He put an arm around Grace, and he said softly: "It's like we said the other night. We've lived our lives. Nothing ahead but rheumatism. Now you stiffen up your lip."

She stopped crying. While Ed dug the grave, she sat on the grass beside Hamp's body, holding his limp hand. Later they lowered his body into the grave, but before Ed started to shovel dirt into the hole, she said—"Wait."—and, lifting her face to the cloud-draped sky, she recited the Lord's Prayer. Then she whispered: "Receive his soul, dear God, and forgive his sins which were so few."

She turned and walked back to the camp. Lowe swallowed, his lips trembling, then he followed her. For a time Ed didn't move. He leaned on his shovel handle, staring across the mesa, the divide to the north hidden by the clouds. You never really knew about people, he thought, not until a time like this came to them. He had not supposed Grace knew the Lord's Prayer, but she had gone through it, slowly and reverently, not stumbling over a single word. Whatever God Who was up there behind those clouds was like, it would be all right with Hamp.

Ed filled in the grave, making a long, red mound, and, finding a smooth, flat rock, set it at the head of the grave. When he returned to camp, he expected to find the horses saddled, the camp gear packed, but nothing had been done.

"We ain't going," Lowe said, his face set stubbornly.

"They'll come," Grace cried. "You may be next, Billy. We've got to go." She looked at Ed, her eyes begging him. "Tell him."

"No one's tellng me anything," Lowe said harshly. "You go if you want to, but I'm staying. Sure they'll come, so I'm waiting. All I'm asking for is that Dal Barger will be with 'em."

# Chapter Fifteen

Carrying the shovel, Ed walked toward the windfall, not wanting to argue. He knew how Lowe felt. The two old men had been together for years, and, if Lowe went back to Gateway House with Grace, his life would never be the same without Hamp. Probably he would prefer death. The dislike Ed had felt for Lowe was gone. He was tough and evil-tempered and harsh of tongue, but he loved Grace. There could be no doubt of that.

When Ed reached the uprooted tree, he studied it for a time, having no faith that this was the right place. There was no telling how long the pine had been down. It had been thrown against its neighbor, stripping limbs from one side of the standing tree and giving it a fantastic, half-bodied appearance. The windfall and the limbs that it had torn from the other pine lay in a tangled mass.

If the money had been buried here, it must be under the trunk of the windfall. Ed got to work, digging along the trunk. Splintered fragments of limbs were driven into the ground; he had to dig them out and kick them aside. He might have to work back on the other side of the trunk, and, if he did, it would be an all-day job.

He struck a large slab of rock that could not be moved because the full weight of the trunk was on it. He swore angrily, frustration working into him. There was no way to tell how much time they had, perhaps a few hours, or all day, depending on where Barger and his crew were. He scooped dirt and needles from the rock, found the other side, and went on digging.

The storm held off, but the thunder was ominously close, the lightning crackling overhead. It was dangerous, working this close to a standing tree, but he could not quit. He was not aware that Grace stood beside him until she said: "Dinner's ready."

He stopped and turned to her. "Can't stop. If it ain't here, we're licked, but I aim to make sure it ain't here before we give up."

Looking at her grief-lined face, he realized how heavily the sense of guilt lay upon her. She was close to the breaking point; the cold determination that had ruled her for so long was gone. She stared at the flat slab of rock as if she didn't see it.

"Nothing makes any difference now, Ed," she said. "Not to me, but I'll stay as long as you want to." She swallowed. "I feel like Billy. About Barger, I mean. I guess you think I'm crazy. Maybe I am. I thought I hated him, but I didn't. Not until Hamp was killed." She licked dry lips. "But I hate him now."

He went on digging. He said: "What you've been saying about leaving to get away from Barger doesn't make any sense when you know he's pulling up stakes, too."

"It wasn't just getting away from him." She kept on staring moodily at the rock. "What it really amounted to was getting away from everything that reminded me of Barger, but that isn't necessary now. He killed Hamp just as much as if he was the one who pulled the trigger."

Ed kept on forcing the shovel into the hard, red soil, making a two-foot trench along the trunk. She was crazy, he thought, or willful. Probably her father had spoiled her, letting her have her way in everything, and, after he died, Hamp and Billy Lowe and Lissa had gone on catering to her whims. Barger, with his grand manner and gifted tongue, had appealed to her, and, when she had realized he was drifting away from her, she had not been willing to give him up, so she had gone on trying to satisfy him because she could not bear the thought of failure.

"I'll bring your dinner," she said.

Still she tarried, staring at the slab of rock as if unable to tear her eyes away from it. Presently she said in a low voice: "I kept wondering how Ben would have buried that money. He knew Barger would hunt for it, and, if there was any sign of fresh digging, Barger would find it."

Ed straightened and leaned on the shovel handle. "What kind of an idea have you got in your head?"

"Well, he'd figure out some way to hide his digging. Maybe he dug a hole and buried the saddlebags, then laid that rock on it, and scooped needles. . . ."

"Hell's bells," Ed said softly. "Why didn't I think of that?"

He started digging under the slab. The dirt was loose and mixed with pine needles. "I think you hit on it," Ed said excitedly. "This ain't as hard as the dirt I've been digging. Of course, dirt will settle in four years, but you wouldn't find pine needles."

He threw the shovel down and dropped to his knees. He started digging with his hands, and Grace, catching his excitement, knelt beside him. "You've got it!" she screamed. "That's a saddlebag."

The leather was visible now. Ed tugged at it and swore when he couldn't budge it. Grace jumped up and called: "Billy, come here. We've found it."

Lowe had remained at the fire. Now he started toward them. "I won't believe it till I see it."

A rifle cracked from the willows along the creek, and Lowe spun and fell. Ed dropped flat on his stomach as three men started running toward them from the creek. He grabbed Grace's hand and pulled her down. She screamed: "They shot Billy! I've got to go to him!"

"Stay here." Ed pulled his gun. "You can't do him any good."

He held her arm, forcing her to be beside him. She quit struggling and began to cry hysterically, whispering: "They got Billy, too."

There was nothing Ed could do but lie belly-flat. If he poked his head over the pine trunk, he'd get it shot off. Then cold fear rammed its fingers into his middle. They had Winchesters, and he had only his Colt. Hamp's and Lowe's rifles were back at the fire, thirty yards away. They might as well have been thirty miles.

"We're in a tight," he said hoarsely. "A hell of a tight. All that they've got to do is to work around to this side and stay out of the range of my six-gun. Hell, it'll be like shooting ducks on a pond."

"I'll get the rifles!" she cried. "They won't shoot me."

"Stay here!" he shouted. "They'd shoot you same as they would me."

He still held her arm with his left hand, afraid to let go. Sweat broke through his skin. He couldn't hear them coming, but any sound they'd make would be covered by the thunder. They had him pinned. They could wait. He wondered if Barger was with them. He'd had only a glimpse, but none of them looked like Barger.

"Morgan!" a man yelled between claps of thunder.

He wasn't far. Ed didn't answer. Lightning broke out into a great, quivering burst of fire, and thunder shook the earth again. Ed lay there, right hand gripping gun butt. He thought of crawling toward the roots of the tree and lunging around it. He might get one of them, if he was lucky, but one wouldn't do.

"Morgan!" the man yelled again. "Throw your gun over the tree and stand up. If you've got the money, we'll make a deal."

Still Ed didn't move, and he didn't say anything. Some men were incapable of waiting. They might rush him. If they did, he had a chance. Again lightning licked out across the sky, thunder coming immediately after the flash, and, as it died, Ed heard a rifle crack. From somewhere on the rim. Not close enough to be any of Barger's riders. Another man was buying into the fight.

Again the rifle cracked, and a man screamed in agony. Ed would never have a better time. He said—"Stay here."—and crawled along the trunk. As he reached it, a third shot came from the rim, then, hammer back, he peered around the root end of the windfall. Two men lay not far from where Billy Lowe had fallen, a third was running along the creek.

Ed fired, but the man went on. Ed sprinted after him, yelling at him to stop, but the man kept going. Again Ed threw a shot. He got the man in the leg, dropping him in a sprawling heap. The fellow lost his gun. He grabbed for it, but Ed was close now. He got the man in the chest with his third shot. He fell flat, his face in the dirt.

The man was not dead when Ed reached him. He rolled him over on his back. A stranger, a young man, probably one of Barger's riders who had been brought down from the cow camp. He stared at Ed, blood drooling from the corners of his mouth.

"Where's Barger?" he demanded.

"He's coming," the man said. "He's got the rest of the boys. He'll get you."

"Have you been here all the time?"

"No. We were coming from the ranch and saw Clark Delaney's horse. We knew you'd got him, so one of the boys went back to get Barger."

Delaney must have been the man who had killed Hamp. Ed asked: "How many men has Barger got?"

"Enough." The fellow's eyes were glazed with death. He labored for breath, and said again—"Enough . . ."—and then he was gone.

Ed wheeled back. Grace was cradling Billy Lowe's head on her lap, and, when Ed came up to her, she stared at him, dry-eyed. There were no more tears in her, he thought. First Hamp, now Billy Lowe. She didn't say anything. She just sat there, staring at Lowe's slack face, too numb to feel anything.

Ed got the shovel from the windfall, and, when he came back to her, he saw that two riders were coming down from the rim. For the moment he had forgotten about the help that had come so unexpectedly. He stood staring at them, frozen. The first rider was Spur Gowdy, the second Honey Travers.

He was still standing there when they picked their way down the talus slope and came on to him. They reined up, Gowdy saying easily: "You were in a hole, Morgan."

"Thanks," Ed said, his eyes on Honey.

She stepped stiffly from her horse and stood looking at him, tall and proud as she always was, and yet different. Her face was streaked with dust, her boots scuffed, her blouse and riding skirt stained and torn. She had been out here a long time, he thought. Her hair, which had always been neatly pinned, lay in a tangled yellow mass down her back.

"Are you all right, Ed?" she asked.

"I'm all right." Ed glanced at Gowdy who was watching them closely, his face as bland as ever, then Ed's gaze swung back to Honey. For a moment he was sick with suspicion, his mind prodded by the knowledge that she had been there with Gowdy all this time, and then he said—"Honey."—and the suspicion washed out of his mind, and he took a step toward her, his hands held out, and she came into his arms.

She kissed him, her arms circling him, clutching him with feverish urgency. Then she drew her lips from him, and she whispered: "I didn't know what had happened to you until we saw you ride in here and camp."

"We don't have a hell of a lot of time," Gowdy said sharply. "Did you find the *dinero?*"

"We found it," Ed said. "That's what fetched 'em in."

"Ed." Honey's hands squeezed his arms. "Did you think of me?"

"I thought of nothing else." And once more he was ashamed of the suspicion he had had of her. She had saved his life at Fishhook, and she and Gowdy had saved it again just now. "I thought I'd never see you again."

"I wouldn't go far," she said quickly, "but I never want to live like this again, not knowing what happened to you." She took a long breath. "We left right after you did because we knew what Barger would do. We guessed this was close to where you'd come, so we've been watching from the rim. We kept out of Lowe's sight because we thought we could do more good if nobody knew we were here."

"Where's the *dinero?*" Gowdy demanded.

"Under the windfall," Ed said.

"Morgan," Grace said, "we've got to bury Billy."

"No time," Gowdy said brusquely.

"Time enough for burying a good man," Ed said and, turning from Honey, picked up the shovel and walked around Hamp's grave.

The rain came then, suddenly, a vicious downpour that soaked all of them in the first minute. Ed worked at the grave with feverish haste, glancing occasionally at Gowdy, who had found the saddlebags of money and had carried them to the camp.

Then Honey came to Ed, and she said: "We'll saddle up. Spur says the only thing we can do is to strike out west and try to get into Utah. Otherwise, we'll have to fight all of Barger's men."

He nodded and went on digging, water coming into the grave. A hell of a way to bury a man, but it was all they could do. Grace was still holding Billy Lowe's head in her lap, and, when Ed walked over to her, she said: "Is it over, Ed? Will it ever be over?"

"It's not over yet," Ed said. "We've got to save ourselves if we can."

He carried Lowe's body to the grave and lowered it into the shallow water, hoping Grace would not know the water was there. If she did, she gave no sign. Once more she recited the Lord's Prayer and whirled away, choked now by the tears that she could not shed before.

Honey put her arms around Grace, and they walked back to the camp. It took time to fill the grave, for the dirt was mud now and stuck to the shovel. When Ed was done, he was weak with weariness, but he hunted until he found another slab of rock and marked the grave. Then he walked to where Gowdy held the horses.

"Ready?" the gunman asked, his voice showing his bitterness over this waste of time.

"Ready," Ed said. "Where's the money?"

"In your saddlebags," Gowdy said. "I thought I'd better move it. Ben's weren't in good shape, being buried so long."

"I'm going home," Grace said.

"You can't!" Honey cried. "You'll run into Barger. You don't know Barger, not the way I do."

"That's right," Gowdy said. "By this time he's out of his head. Failure is something he can't stand, and he's had too many failures since Ed Morgan got clear of the trap he set for him on the San Miguel."

"I don't care . . . ," Grace began.

"You're coming with us," Ed said.

She didn't argue. She had no spirit for it. He gave Grace a

hand as she mounted, and then he saw that Honey was already in the saddle.

Gowdy mounted, laughing softly. "Morgan, I never took you for a sentimental man, but, by damn, taking time that may mean our lives to bury a corpse is nothing but fool sentiment."

Ed said nothing as he swung aboard his buckskin. He was wet and chilled and so tired that the choice between living and dying didn't seem to matter. The rain had stopped, the storm moving northward, and, as they turned their horses toward the creek, the western sky was bright blue. It wasn't until they had splashed across the stream that a question occurred to Ed about the money. He wondered if it really was in his saddlebags, or in Gowdy's.

# Chapter Sixteen

There was a stretch of open country beyond the creek. Looking northward, Ed could see nothing but the rain that was a black curtain drawn across the mesa. He shivered, his wet clothes clinging to him. The wind was strong in his face, cold and damp. Both girls, he thought, must be utterly miserable.

Grace was ahead of him, riding beside Gowdy, her head bent. She was past caring about anything. She'd had her greedy dream; she had bargained for half the money, but she hadn't given any thought to the price she would pay. Now only Lissa was left.

He glanced at Honey, who was looking at him, smiling, her blue-green eyes bright and filled with pleasure at being with him again. The rain had washed her face clean, her hair was wet and matted, but in spite of her bedraggled appearance she still seemed beautiful to him.

Suddenly he laughed, the first time he had laughed for a long time. He felt good, wonderfully good, now that Honey was here beside him. She hadn't said in words that she loved him and not Gowdy, but he knew. He had been jealous, foolishly jealous, but now that was behind him.

"Do I look that funny?" she asked.

He shook his head. "You don't look funny at all. I just felt like laughing."

Her face was grave then. She tipped her head toward Gowdy in a short nod, and said in a tone so low that he barely heard: "Watch him, Ed. He's talked about wanting big money as long as I've known him. He won't miss this chance."

His mind had been so completely on Barger that he had

not given any thought to why Gowdy had been waiting up there on the rim. He hadn't even been clear in his own mind why Gowdy had helped him get way from Fishhook, or what sort of deal Honey had made with him. Now, with that nod of her head, he knew. Gowdy wanted the money, and Gowdy was as dangerous as Dal Barger with all his men.

Ed's gun was in his holster. He drew it, ejected the empty shells, thumbed new leads into the cylinder, and then slid his gun back into leather. Gowdy had a Winchester in the scabbard, and Ed saw that Honey was carrying one, too. He swore softly, remembering that they had left Hamp's and Billy Lowe's rifles on the other side of the creek.

"We've got plenty of shells," Honey said in the same low tone, "and I have a small revolver I found in Barger's desk. Gowdy won't make any trouble until he knows we're out of Barger's reach."

Ed nodded, remembering that in their haste to start moving they hadn't once thought to bring any grub. There would be no ranches on this side of the mountains, but somewhere beyond them in the west they'd find the Utah town of Moab. He didn't know where it was, and he doubted that Honey did. They'd go hungry, that was sure, but it was Gowdy, not starvation, he feared. Gowdy! If it came to a showdown fight between them, he had no chance against a professional gunman like Spur Gowdy.

Suddenly Gowdy raised a hand and pointed north, swearing bitterly. Ed turned his head. The storm had moved on toward the Diablo, and now a band of riders was in sight.

"You and your burying!" Gowdy shouted. "Barger's got a Ute cowhand who can trail a grasshopper across a rock."

"How far are we from the Utah line?" Ed asked.

"Too far to beat 'em to it," he snapped, "even if it would do any good."

Gowdy brought his horse into a run, the others keeping pace with him, and a moment later they were among rocks again, the same kind of barren country they had traversed before they had reached the campsite. Ed glanced north. Barger's bunch was coming fast.

They started the climb into the hills, and Gowdy had to pull his horse down to a walk. If there was a fight, it might as well be here, Ed thought, but Gowdy apparently wanted no part of it. They angled up a cedar-covered ridge, dropped down the other side, and climbed another, higher than the first. Barger's men were not in sight now, but by that time they must have reached the boulders at the base of the first ridge.

The sun, well to the west now, was hot upon a wet earth, its slanting light sharp and glaring. Their clothes would soon be dry, Ed thought absently, and he wondered what Gowdy planned. The chance of outriding Barger's men seemed a dim one.

They topped the second ridge and looked down upon a chocolate-brown river. "The Dolores," Honey said. "We've got to ford it. We'll hit an old Ute trail down there. Barger used to send outlaws this way. Spur guided them."

So Gowdy knew the country, Ed thought, probably better than Barger did, but Barger had an Indian with him who was even more familiar with the country than Gowdy was. They headed directly down the slope to the river and swung upstream, Gowdy glancing back, his face dour. Ed had never seen him look like this before. He had seemed indifferent, a bland man who had a gift for hiding his feelings, but he wasn't hiding them now. He was scared. It puzzled Ed who for some reason felt no fear at all. He must be numb, he told himself.

A man can be scared just so long, he thought. Or maybe he was too tired to feel anything. He glanced at Honey, who had dropped behind. She gave him a quick smile. A lot of woman, this Honey Travers, more woman than Ben had ever guessed. Remembering how she had looked that night at Fishhook in her pretty dress, he found it hard to believe that this was the same Honey Travers.

They found the trail and forded the river, which ran swiftly here over a smooth, sandstone bottom, the silt-laden water belly-high on their horses. They reached the opposite bank and swung up on the ridge, the trail looping back and forth between points of rock. Just as they reached the top, a rifle cracked from the river below them, the bullet snapping past within a foot of Ed's head, then they were over the hump and going down the other side.

"Why don't we make a stand?" Ed called. "Plenty of cover here."

Gowdy looked back, his face ugly, and he cursed Ed with vicious venom. "You and your god-damned burying!" he shouted. "Shut up now!"

Not much daylight left, for the sun was beginning to settle behind the next hill. The Utah line could not be far ahead, but a state line would not turn Barger.

Ed had never seen more desolate country—a sparse stand of grama grass and shad scale and a few cedars, and rocks, fat ones, and jagged points, and innumerable piles of slab rock. There were places in the trail where the thin soil had been washed away so that hoofs pounded with a great clatter on the solid sandstone.

Again they reached the ridge top, and again a rifle cracked as they were briefly silhouetted against the sky. They started down the switchbacks once more. More ridges were ahead, a jumbled, criss-crossed pattern, the mountains hidden by them.

By the time they reached the bottom and had climbed

halfway to the top of the next ridge, it was apparent that Barger's men were cutting down the distance between them. Running was foolish, it seemed to Ed, for now several rifles opened up, bullets hammering into the rocks around them and screaming away into space.

Gowdy swore savagely. Jerking his Winchester from the boot, he turned in his saddle and fired three times at the men behind them who were clearly visible on the ridge crest to the east. Glancing back, Ed saw one rider spill out of the saddle as the rest scattered in spite of Barger's flaying voice, which carried across the cañon.

"Come on!" Gowdy bawled, and put his horse on up the slope.

There was no more firing until they reached the top, then there was a single wild shot. Poor shooting, Ed thought. Or it might have been purposely bad. Barger didn't want the women hit. Not Honey, anyhow. Gowdy must have realized now that running was not the answer, for when they reached the bottom of the cañon, he swung off the trail and headed south, following the narrow, rock-strewn trough.

Within fifty yards the walls of the cañon became precipices. Another half mile and Ed saw they weren't going any farther. They were in a box cañon, the slick rock rims two hundred feet above them jutting toward each other so that the sky was a narrow, blue ribbon.

Gowdy pulled up and swung down. "You wanted to stop and fight, Morgan," he said. "All right, you'll get a bellyful." He yanked the Winchester from the boot with a violent motion. "Not much water and less grub. All Barger's got to do is wait us out." He swallowed, his face anything but bland now, then added: "You and your god-damned burying."

Ed dismounted and gave Honey a hand. Grace almost fell out of her saddle. She gripped the horn and steadied herself, then she made it to a flat rock. Ed led the horses to the back of the cañon where they would be protected from stray bullets by a point of sandstone that jutted out from the sheer wall. He stripped gear from them and tied them to some cedars that somehow found precarious footing in what looked like solid rock. Honey helped move the saddles and canteens to the base of a boulder, then they returned to where Gowdy stood staring in the direction Barger must come.

"Did you ever count them, Spur?" Honey asked.

Ed wondered why she asked, for she had probably counted Barger's men herself, but apparently the gunman found nothing unusual in the question. He said: "Six. There was seven, but I got one of 'em."

"That was a good shot," Honey said.

Gowdy gave her a questioning glance. Ed understood then. She was bolstering the gunman's courage! A strange thing, Ed thought. A man like Gowdy could be brave under some circumstances and a coward under others. This business of being shoved into a corner was not to his liking.

"Yeah, it was a fair shot," Gowdy said uncertainly.

"We're pretty well fixed," Honey said. "If they rush us, they'll think they ran into something."

"They'll wait," Gowdy muttered. "We can't go no farther, and they know it."

"How would Barger know that?" Honey asked.

Gowdy seemed surprised. "Hell, maybe he don't. I'm not sure he's got that Ute. If he hasn't, he won't know, and they'll come piling into us. They might even go on up the trail."

"I hope they come," Ed said.

Honey handed her Winchester to Ed, saying: "I expect you're a better shot than I am. I'll lay out the shells."

She went back to where they had left the saddlebags. Gowdy said in a low voice: "This is a good time to make one

180

thing clear. If we get out of this alive, the fifty thousand's mine."

Gowdy would be very brave against a single man like Ed who worked for a living instead of hiring his gun. Now, staring at him, Ed saw that his face had assumed its natural blandness again. Ed was remembering when he had first seen Gowdy that night in Gateway House. The man had ruthlessly built his reputation. Once he had established it, he used fear to gain his ends, but backed into a corner, he was just another frightened man.

"To hell with you," Ed snapped. "Grace gets half of the money. I made a bargain with her."

"It'll take all of it to satisfy me, bucko," Gowdy said. "Why do you think I killed Riddle? And took chips today back there on the rim? Hell, it wasn't because I love you. I love the fifty thousand."

"Maybe you had some notions about Honey."

"I did, but I lost them."

"I'll divvy up," Ed said, "but I made a deal with Grace, and I'll keep my bargain. Say, where is she?"

He had not realized she was gone until he looked around for her. "I don't know," Gowdy said, "but it's her business, if she wants to walk out of here."

He knew, all right, Ed thought. She'd gone back down the cañon, and Gowdy had let her go, not caring what happened to her and undoubtedly guessing, before Ed had told him, that Grace had helped Ed for part of the money. Swearing, Ed started down the cañon, paying no attention to Gowdy, who shouted at him to stay where he was.

Ed had not gone fifty feet before he saw Barger's men riding toward him. He ducked behind a boulder, edged around it, and lunged toward another one. They saw him then. A rifle cracked from the man in the lead, and a long series of echoes were thrown back by the cañon walls.

Then he realized what a damned fool thing he had done. He couldn't hold off six of them by himself. Sooner or later they'd pick him off, and then there would be just Gowdy and the two girls.

# Chapter Seventeen

There was no way to tell how far Grace had gone, or where she was now. Ed pulled his gun and sprinted toward the next boulder, drawing another bullet that hit a rock and screamed as it ricocheted through space. Barger's men had dismounted and were working their way toward him. The Ute tracker must be with them, Ed thought.

For a moment he remained behind the boulder, mentally condemning himself for acting on a sudden impulse. But Grace was out here somewhere. The deaths of Lowe and Hamp, the storm, and their fight must have made her go out of her mind. Then another thought came to him. Perhaps she had gone over to Barger, making the one last frantic effort to regain his love.

He heard her call out from somewhere up ahead. Ed slid to the side of the boulder, his back pressed against it, eyes searching the talus slope at the foot of the sandstone wall. A minute or more passed before he made out her small figure, and in the thin light he saw that she had a gun in her hand.

As he watched her, Ed saw fire spurt from the muzzle of her gun, and, before the echoes of the shot died, he heard her scream: "That was for Hamp, Barger!" She was out in the open, an easy target for the Fishhook men. Ed ran forward. He saw one of Barger's riders line his rifle on Grace; he cut down the man with his first shot.

Once more Grace fired. She cried out: "That was for Billy, Barger!"

She dropped flat as other guns sounded. Barger's men had moved around the rocks they were using for cover to get out of the range of her Colt. Now they were caught between her fire and Ed's. With Barger down, they wasted no more of it.

They started to run, panicky now, and Ed got one before they reached their horses, sending him down in a headlong fall.

Grace began firing again, her shots adding to their panic. Three of them were on their feet, but as they swung into saddles, Ed emptied his gun, knocking another one out of leather. The other two went thundering down the cañon.

Ed ejected the empties from his gun and loaded as he ran forward. Barger lay on his back, eyes staring unseeingly at the darkening sky. Grace was standing over him, the empty gun in her hand at her side, tears running down her cheeks.

She lifted her eyes to Ed. "It's over now. I had to do it for Hamp and Billy." She gripped Ed's arm. "Do they know what I've just done? Will they forgive me for killing them? I did, you know."

She hadn't, not the way Ed looked at it, but he sensed she did not want to be persuaded, so he said simply: "Sure they know, and they'll forgive you."

She rubbed her eyes with the knuckles of her left hand like a little girl. She said again: "It's over now."

She had saved all their lives, but that was not important to her. Ed said: "Yeah, that finished it."

"They didn't see me," Grace said. "I waited behind a rock, and they were below me, and then I shot him."

She was beyond thinking, beyond feeling. Ed had only sympathy for her as he looked at her blank, frozen face. Then he remembered that two of them were still alive. They would probably keep on going, but there was a chance they wouldn't, if they knew the money had been found.

"Honey!" Ed shouted. "Gowdy! Bring the horses." He gave Grace a push. "Go back and help them. Tell them to hurry."

He ran on down the cañon, hearing the receding drum of hoofs, but before he reached the trail, he knew they had turned back toward Fishhook. He waited, breathing hard, thinking about Gowdy and wondering what the man would do.

It was almost dark when they came, Honey leading Ed's buckskin. Gowdy was in the lead. He pulled up as Ed mounted. He said: "You're quite a hero, Morgan. Nobody but a hero would go out there to save a woman."

"Let's ride," Ed said.

Honey was now behind Gowdy, a small pistol pointed at his back. If the man was aware of it, he gave no sign. He went on, and, when he reached the trail, he turned west along it. They rode single file for an hour, the sky clear and filled with stars. No one talked until they reached a small, grassy valley tucked in between two hills.

"No use riding till sunup." Gowdy reined up. "How many got away, Morgan?"

"Two."

"They won't come back," he said, and dismounted.

For a moment neither Honey nor Ed moved, not sure what Gowdy meant to do. He off-saddled and staked his horse out, then Ed stepped down. He asked Honey: "What will he do now?"

"I don't know," she whispered. "I never know about him."

"We'd better rest," Ed said.

He gave her a hand, and, when she had dismounted and stood beside him, she said: "I don't think he'll do anything tonight. There's only one thing that's predictable about him. He brags about always giving the other man his chance."

Ed pulled off the saddles. "Stay here," he said, and led the horses away. Gowdy had stretched on the ground, his head on his saddle. Ed went back for Grace's horse. *Gone to sleep, maybe,* Ed thought. *Looks like we've jumped out of the frying pan into the fire.*

Grace was on the ground, holding her head in her hands. Ed brought her saddle and blanket to her, and, when he returned from staking out her horse, Honey had persuaded Grace to lie down and had covered her with the blanket.

"I'm not sleeping tonight," Ed said.

"You'd better," Honey said. "I'll stay awake."

He knew what she meant. Tomorrow Gowdy would force a fight upon him. Tonight he needed his rest. But it wouldn't make any difference. He couldn't outdraw Gowdy. He'd have to find some other way. But when he lay down, he found that he could not stay awake, and it seemed that he had only dropped off to sleep when Honey shook him awake, whispering: "It's almost daylight, Ed." He sat up, rubbing his eyes, and it was a moment before his mind was cleared of the fog of sleep.

"Spur's still asleep," Honey whispered. "You might be able to get his gun."

Gowdy's body was a motionless mound under his blanket. Ed considered this. Even if he got Gowdy's gun and Winchester, it would settle nothing, for the man would follow. Only death would stay him.

"He told me once that fifty thousand dollars was enough to corrupt all of us," Honey whispered. "He's right. It's brought nothing but trouble. Why don't we let him have it?"

"Half goes to Grace," Ed said. "I made a deal with her, and Gowdy wants all of it."

He rose. It was better to make his try now, he thought. If he could disarm Gowdy, they could ride without worrying about what the man would do. Postponement. That was all. But something might happen.

He drew his gun and moved slowly toward Gowdy, wondering how sound a sleeper the man was. He had his answer at once, for he was still ten feet from Gowdy when he caught the movement of Gowdy's hand under the blanket.

The shot came an instant later, a great roar in the silence, and Ed felt the searing pain of the bullet as it sliced along his side. He fired, the slug catching Gowdy in his left shoulder. Gowdy shot through the blanket again, but he missed completely, and Ed's second bullet ripped through his chest.

Ed stood over him, his gun pointed at Gowdy's head. The gunman whispered: "Never bet aces when you're playing the other man's game. I should have made you play mine. Should have killed you . . . last . . . night."

Ed heard Grace's long-drawn scream. He knew that Honey was standing beside him and heard her ask: "Are you all right?"

"Lost some hide," Ed said. "Gowdy's dead, and for no good reason. It wouldn't have gone this way if he'd settled for less than all of it."

They rode through scrub oak and serviceberry brush that day, a steady climb to the top, not stopping until they reached a spring in a bunch of aspens. They watered their horses, then ate sparingly of the cold biscuits and jerky that Honey carried in her saddlebags. After they had finished eating, Ed took a look at the money, most of it greenbacks wrapped in pieces of a yellow slicker. Four years in the ground had not hurt it.

"We'll count it and make an even split when we get to Moab," he told Grace.

She looked at him in the strange, blank way she had, then said listlessly: "All right."

Ed rose. He thought of what the money had done to Ben; to Barger who had not needed it but could not stand the failure that losing it represented; to Gowdy who, waking suddenly, had become panicky when he saw Ed coming toward him and had lost his head; and to Grace who had paid too high a price for her share of it.

"It's no good, is it, Honey?" he asked. "It'll never do us any good."

"We can do some good with it," she said. "I don't want it, but we'll find somebody that it will do good for."

He walked away through the aspens, and she caught up with him and took his arm. "Ed, I want to tell you something. I couldn't tell you at Fishhook because you wouldn't believe me, but you will now, won't you?"

"I love you," he said. "You have to believe in the woman you love. I've gone through a lot of hell the last few days to learn it."

She smiled. "I like to hear that." Then her face was grave. "When I told you to come to Fishhook, I was sure I could handle Barger. I thought it was the only way I could save your life. I knew, if you went after it yourself, he'd kill you. You see, he promised not to harm you, if he got the ten thousand he said he had coming, but I know now he never intended to keep that promise. He'd always kept his word before." She gestured wearily. "Well, it shows what a lot of money will do even to a man who didn't need it."

He looked at her, believing her and loving her, and wanting her to see it in his face. Whatever was past was gone, and the future was theirs, and he would never doubt her again.

"I've made a lot of mistakes," she said, "but the biggest one was with Ben. I was wrong, and I wanted nice things, so he set out to get them for me. Every time I went to see him in prison, we quarreled because he didn't believe in me. I changed during those four years, Ed. He couldn't understand that. Then when he wrote that he was coming and for me to meet him at Gateway House. . . ." She lowered her head, unable to look at Ed. "Well, you know about that. All I could think of was to prove to him I loved him."

"Will I do for a husband?" he asked. "Being second choice doesn't worry me."

She did look at him, then, her head held in the proud way he liked. "Of course, you'll do. You're not second choice, you know. I never felt about Ben the way I do about you."

He kissed her, and she put her arms around him, and clung to him as if she could never let him go.

# About the Author

Wayne D. Overholser won three Golden Spur awards from the Western Writers of America and has a long list of fine Western titles to his credit. He was born in Pomeroy, Washington, and attended the University of Montana, University of Oregon, and the University of Southern California before becoming a public schoolteacher and principal in various Oregon communities. He began writing for Western pulp magazines in 1936 and within a couple of years was a regular contributor to Street & Smith's *Western Story Magazine* and Fiction House's *Lariat Story Magazine*. BUCKAROO'S CODE (1947) was his first Western novel and remains one of his best. In the 1950s and 1960s, having retired from academic work to concentrate on writing, he would publish as many as four books a year under his own name or a pseudonym, most prominently as Joseph Wayne. THE VIOLENT LAND (1954), THE LONE DEPUTY (1957), THE BITTER NIGHT (1961), and RIDERS OF THE SUNDOWNS (1997) are among the finest of the Overholser titles. THE SWEET AND BITTER LAND (1950), BUNCH GRASS (1955), and LAND OF PROMISES (1962) are among the best Joseph Wayne titles, and LAW MAN (1953) is a most rewarding novel under the pseudonym Lee Leighton. Overholser's Western novels, whatever the byline, are based on a solid knowledge of the history and customs of the 19th-Century West, particularly when set in his two favorite Western states, Oregon and Colorado. Many of his novels are first-person narratives, a technique that tends to bring an added dimension of vividness to the frontier experiences of his narrators and frequently, as in CAST A LONG SHADOW (1957), the female characters one en-

190

counters are among the most memorable. He wrote his numerous novels with a consistent skill and an uncommon sensitivity to the depths of human character. Almost invariably, his stories weave a spell of their own with their scenes and images of social and economic forces often in conflict and the diverse ways of life and personalities that made the American Western frontier so unique a time and place in human history. RAINBOW RIDER will be his next **Five Star Western**.